Dear Reader,

Home, family, community and love. These are the values we cherish most in our lives—the ideals that ground us, comfort us, move us. They certainly provide the perfect inspiration around which to build a romance collection that will touch the heart.

And so we are thrilled to offer you the Harlequin Heartwarming series. Each of these special stories is a wholesome, heartfelt romance imbued with the traditional values so important to you. They are books you can share proudly with friends and family. And the authors featured in this collection are some of the most talented storytellers writing today, including favorites such as Roz Denny Fox, Margaret Daley and Mary Anne Wilson. We've selected these stories especially for you based on their overriding qualities of emotion and tenderness, and they center on your favorite themes—children, weddings, second chances, the reunion of families, the quest to find a true home and, of course, sweet romance.

So curl up in your favorite chair, relax and prepare for a heartwarming reading experience!

Sincerely,

The Editors

MARY ANNE WILSON

is a Canadian transplanted to Southern California, where she lives with her husband, three children and an assortment of animals.

She knew she wanted to write romances when she found herself "rewriting" the great stories in literature, such as *A Tale of Two Cities,* to give them "happy endings." Over her long career she's published more than thirty romances, had her books on bestseller lists, been nominated for Reviewer's Choice Awards and received a career nomination in romantic suspense.

HARLEQUIN HEARTWARMING

Mary Anne Wilson

For the Love of Hayley

Recycling programs
for this product may
not exist in your area.

ISBN-13: 978-0-373-36614-9

FOR THE LOVE OF HAYLEY

Copyright © 2013 by Mary Anne Wilson

Originally published as WINNING SARA'S HEART
Copyright © 2004 by Mary Anne Wilson

Printed in U.S.A.

H HARLEQUIN®
www.Harlequin.com

For the Love of Hayley

For Linda

CHAPTER ONE

E. J. SOMMERS didn't want to be here. He wanted to be anywhere but in the limousine heading into downtown Houston for a meeting at LynTech. He didn't want to sit in some stuffy conference room, facing the head honchos across a shiny table and negotiate away part of his own company. If it were up to him, he'd be out somewhere in the open, alone, letting his attorney take care of the whole thing.

"Everything okay?" Martin Griggs, that very same attorney, asked. "You look…" His voice trailed off.

E.J. turned to Martin, a thin man in a perfectly tailored, pin-striped navy suit, and with much less red hair than he'd had ten years ago when he'd first come on board with the newly formed EJS Corporation. "Just how do I look?" he asked, his dark hazel eyes narrowing on the man.

"As if you'd rather be drawn and quartered than do this," Martin said without missing a beat.

"Right on the mark," E.J. murmured.

"You need to be in the meeting, to show that the power goes all the way to the top, and you're the one in control."

E.J. nodded. "I know."

"But, you don't look too convinced."

"I'm convinced, but you know I'm never sure of anything in business. I do this by the seat of my pants, not because I've got some impressive degree to hang my opinions and actions on. I never even made it past high school."

"Education or not, by doing it your way, you've been a success, made millions, and have one of the most viable corporations around. That's why LynTech wants this deal to go through."

"Just about everyone else looks at me and wonders when I'm going to fall flat on my face, when I'll go back to where I belong and leave the big league to the big-league players."

Martin smiled. "Sure, but you aren't falling flat on your face, and you're here, so they'll deal with you or there won't be a deal at all."

E.J. knew that Martin was stating the facts, but he still wondered what he was doing in this situation to begin with. He'd never set out to be rich, to have this kind of power or influence, and he was willing to let part of his company go to try to make his life simpler. Maybe even to figure out where his life was going from here. What he knew was, he needed time and breathing space, and getting LynTech to take over part of his operations meant he'd get what he wanted.

LynTech would get the high-tech branch of EJS Corporation, freeing him up. Quietly, they were negotiating, and it would be a done deal before the rest of the business world knew what was happening. No sharks would go after EJS Corporation. Just a quiet, fast deal. Those were the rules Jackson Ford, the negotiator for LynTech, had agreed to.

"They'll deal with me," he muttered, and tugged at the cuffs of the brown leather bomber jacket he was wearing over a plain white T-shirt with blue jeans and his favorite pair of boots.

"You know, you really are a legend in the business world," Martin said.

"Oh, sure," he said, almost laughing.

E.J. knew how he was seen by most people. By virtue of his success and his wealth, women pursued him passionately and men went after his holdings. His business opponents were passionately resentful of what they perceived to be his ability to do what they did, but with a deceptive ease that rankled them. "A cocky upstart with an attitude" was one of the kinder remarks he'd heard. He ignored the worst remarks that labeled him as a man who didn't know a contract from his elbow and a man who had more luck than brains.

He knew he'd been lucky in his life. But he'd never apologize for his success. Gossipmongers seemed to thrive on finding out what he was up to.

"Well, Mr. Legend, we're here," Martin said as the limo slowed and pulled to the curb in front of the towering glass-and-metal building that contained LynTech. A security man was there right away, opening E.J.'s door and looking inside.

"Good morning, sir. Can I help you?"

"We're here for a meeting," Martin said. "E. J. Sommers and Martin Griggs."

The khaki-uniformed man, probably in his late twenties, with pale skin and a concerned expression, checked a clipboard he was holding. "Oh, yes, sir," he said with a smile. "The meeting is in the main conference room on the top floor. Mr. Holden said to send you right up when you got here."

Martin's phone rang as E.J. got out, and then the attorney was beside him on the sidewalk, holding up a hand to get E.J's attention. Martin frowned but didn't say anything as he listened to the caller. "Oh, for—" Martin finally muttered, his words stopping abruptly as he listened some more. "This stinks. It's not what we signed on for. I'll be right up," he said, and flipped his phone shut.

"What's going on?" E.J. asked.

"That was Ford. He just found out the deal leaked and the word is on the street. It's making the rounds."

E.J. had actually liked what he'd heard of Ford. When they'd spoken, E.J. got the sense that Ford stood by his word. Had he been mistaken? "What happened?"

"He doesn't know, but it's out and the sharks are circling. It's just what you thought. They're seeing it as a weakness in the structure, and they're going for blood." He motioned to the building. "It's not going to be pretty, but we need to get this done. Come on."

Suddenly a child screamed and E.J. flinched at the piercing sound. He glanced to his left and saw a harried-looking young woman in jeans and a loose T-shirt trying to carry a squirming toddler toward the entrance to the building. "Hush, Walker, Mommy's inside. I promise."

The little boy, with wispy blond hair and

a good set of lungs, let out another ear-piercing scream. "Hush, hush, hush," the woman kept saying as she hurried into the lobby of the LynTech building.

"Sorry, sir," the security man said. "He's going to the day-care center inside. Those kids can be a handful," he said with a shake of his head. "Sure glad I don't have any." Then he realized he might have been out of line and backtracked. "Oh, I'm sorry. I didn't mean that kids are bad or anything. I mean, you each probably have lovely children."

"Two girls," Martin said as he glanced at the closed entry doors. "You say they've got a day-care center in there?"

"Yes, sir. Have for a while now, but I never thought kids should be around business stuff. Just my opinion."

E.J. didn't care about the kids or why a corporation like LynTech would even have children on the premises. He sure didn't want to talk about them or where they should be. Kids didn't matter to him. He didn't care if LynTech had a high school tucked away in the building. What he cared about was a rotten deal, and he didn't want any part of what was waiting for them on the top floor.

"Call Ford back and tell him we're on our way back to Dallas." He wanted complications out of his life. But that wasn't going to happen here and now. "We're cutting our losses and getting out of town."

Martin didn't move. "We can't just walk away without a face-to-face."

"Ford and Holden both promised it was going to be closed, that we wouldn't have to go public with the negotiations."

Martin shook his head. "E.J., in business you have to see things through to the end. You need to tell them—"

"You go and see them if you want to. See what on earth happened, but I'm leaving." Frustration was growing in him, along with impatience. He turned to the security man, who was trying to pretend that he wasn't listening to their conversation. "Where's the nearest place to get a drink?"

"Coffee?" he asked.

When E.J. nodded the man said, "Over there, in the Lennox Building." He motioned to the structure south of LynTech. "They just put in a sort of bar and restaurant on the ground level. Everyone's been saying it's good. Just inside the main doors to the left."

E.J. glanced at a twin to the LynTech Building, all glass and steel with a sweeping entry and the name Lennox carved into a heavy slab of marble used as a cross support over the doors. He turned to Martin. "Give me some cash?"

Martin tucked the phone back in a side pocket of his briefcase, then reached for his wallet. "I wish you'd carry cash, E.J. Do you know how much more bookkeeping I have to do to account for the dribs and drabs you take off me?" he muttered, then looked up at E.J. as he opened his wallet and held it out to him. "Why don't you just take what you need?"

E.J. took a few bills, then said, "Put it on my tab."

"Of course," Martin murmured as he tucked his wallet back in his pocket. "So, you're not coming up with me?"

"No, just let me know when you're ready to head back to Dallas. I'll be at the bar."

Martin nodded, then headed into Lyn-Tech.

"Can my driver stay where he is?" he asked the security man.

"Sure, no problem."

"We should be out of here soon," he said, and was a bit surprised that he felt so let down as he headed toward the next building. He approached the glass doors and caught a flash of his image in the expansive surface. Six feet tall, lean, wearing casual clothes, he didn't look like a company president, not even like an average businessman. At thirty-nine, he was too old to start wearing pin-striped suits and wing-tipped oxfords, and getting razor haircuts.

His brown, sun-streaked hair was a bit too long, a bit too unstyled, and it swept back from a face that was a bit too angular and showed his aversion to shaving, with the shadow of a day-old beard at his strong jaw. He realized he needed that coffee.

He hit the door with the heel of his hand and stepped into a vast reception foyer.

Glass, marble, wood and plants were everywhere. He glanced at a massive information desk to the right, set on a highly polished marble floor.

E.J. caught a hint of brewing coffee in the air and spotted the restaurant entrance. Between two immaculately trimmed topiary plants in brass pots, a frosted-glass wood door was labeled in gold-leaf script. The Lennox Café. He crossed to it, pushed it back and stepped inside. The cold marble and the glass and steel from outside were replaced by plush burgundy carpeting, polished wood and brass, accented with crystal and mirrors.

There was only one customer at the bar and two customers in the restaurant. The man at the bar was reading from his smartphone while nursing a drink, and the other two men were at a round table near tinted windows, talking business with open briefcases in front of them along with drinks.

A slender blond waitress glanced in his direction while she juggled a tray laden with food. Her startling aquamarine eyes dominated a finely boned face that was slightly flushed. "Someone will be right with you," she said in a breathless voice, then headed into the restaurant.

She moved quickly, weaving her way through the empty room, approaching the customers. At the same moment she got to the table, one of the two men pushed his chair back, stood and turned, running right into the waitress. The peace was shattered by the crashing sound of impact, falling food and dishes, a startled scream that probably came from the waitress.

As if everything had shifted to slow motion, E.J. saw the waitress jerk backward and fall out of sight behind the nearest table. The customer took the full brunt of flying food, and a plate bounced off his shoulder before shattering as it hit the edge of the table. A small man, totally bald, with a dark goatee and wearing a somber black suit, rushed toward the table.

The customer stood there, covered with pieces of food and drenched with what had to have been coffee, while his friend, still seated at the table, hurriedly rescued papers and checked them before putting them back in his briefcase. None of the three men gave the waitress more than a cursory glance as she struggled to her feet, her face crimson and her pale hair falling loose in a tangle around her shoulders.

She scrambled up, hurrying to the man who bore the brunt of the disaster, and she reached out to brush at something yellow clinging to his once-immaculate jacket. Before she could do anything to help, the man hit at her hand, thundering, "Let it alone! You've done enough damage."

She drew back quickly, clasping her hands in front of her, then twisting around when the man in the dark suit pulled her back and away from the customer. "Oh, my…oh, goodness," the man said ineffectively in a voice with a slight British accent while he all but pushed the waitress behind him. He never stopped his mantra of apologies and offers of help. "We are so sorry," he was saying. "Just deplorable. Unforgivable. Please, let us make this up to you."

The man standing barely spared him a look while he shrugged out of his jacket, shaking it sharply and sending the clinging food everywhere. One piece of tomato hit the small man in his chest, imprinting a garish red mark on the pristine whiteness of his shirt. He flicked at it, then grabbed a napkin off of a nearby table and proceeded to blot at his shirt. "Sir, this is unforgivable. Please, we will take care of any cleaning bills for your suit."

The irate man turned, red-faced, and said, "It's ruined. It's trash." He dropped the jacket on the table, deliberately setting it on the worst of the mess. "And you *will* take care of it."

"Absolutely, sir. My name is Bernard Hughes and I'm the manager of this establishment. We will make this right, and do accept our profound apology."

The man and his tablemate made to leave. Almost tripping over the waitress's foot, the tall, angry businessman yelled, "Get out of my way, you idiot!" and pushed past her while she crouched down, attending to the mess at her feet.

E.J. wasn't sure when he started to walk toward the disaster, or why he was going in that direction at all. But he was, and the men rushed past him without a glance, muttering something about a meeting.

E.J. approached the manager and the waitress. The polite facade and deference the manager had exuded seconds ago was gone. He reached down, grabbed the waitress by her arm and jerked her unceremoniously to her feet. It was then that he knew why he was heading in their direction.

He'd had enough of everything. The bad deal because of some leak at LynTech, and men who treated this woman as if she was in servitude to the lot of them; they all left a bad taste in his mouth. The taste got even worse when he heard the manager saying, "This is all your fault, you idiot! This is coming out of your pay. And if it happens again, that's it! You are out of here."

He saw the woman's eyes, that incredible shade of aquamarine, the way they widened, and the fear in them. "I...I said I'm sorry," she breathed. "He stood up right when I got here and the tray hit him, and—"

"You threw food all over him," Hughes muttered. "And if he goes out of here and ruins our reputation when we're just getting off the ground, well..." He let the words trail off, but the threat in them was very clear. "The suit cleaning or replacement will be your responsibility completely."

She bit her lip but didn't fight his hold on her or protest anymore. She just stood there, taking it, and that made E.J. all the more angry. He was right by them now, close enough to see a name tag on the woman's dress that read Sara, and close enough to see the pressure the man was putting on her arm. High color dotted her cheeks and she swallowed hard before she whispered, "I am so sorry, sir."

"You will be if you do anything like this again."

"Hey, take it easy," E.J. said, laying his hand on the man's forearm.

Hughes jerked at the contact, looked at E.J., then seemed to relax when he saw a customer. "Excuse me, sir?"

"Let her go," E.J. said, not raising his voice but holding the man's gaze without wavering. "Whatever happened here, it was an accident. I saw that idiot stand up right in front of her, and as far as I could tell, he caused all of this."

Hughes stared at E.J., mentally trying to figure out what in the world was going on. He flicked his gaze over the casual clothes, the roughness on his unshaven jaw, then looked right at him. The deference he'd shown to the other men was there, but in a measured portion. He wasn't going to offend a prospective customer by telling him to get lost, but he wasn't about to just let E.J. run roughshod over him, either.

"Sir, this has nothing to do with you, no matter whose fault it was," he said tightly. "We at the Lennox Café expect excellence from our employees, and if that is no longer the case, they are no longer employees." He inclined his head to E.J. "I can assure you that your service will be impeccable."

"Great, but let go of her," E.J. said.

Red flushed through the man's skin again all the way up to his bald head, but he let the waitress go. "Get this cleaned up, then come to my office," he said to her before he looked back at E.J., clasping his hands in front of his chest to partially hide the red stain there. The man was furious about everything, but he was controlled. "Now, sir, the bar or the restaurant?" he asked tightly.

"The bar."

"Yes, sir, this way," Hughes said, and swept his hand in the direction of the bar.

E.J. glanced at the waitress. She had dropped to her haunches again and was busily scooping the ruined food back onto the tray. He leaned toward her. "Are you okay?"

She looked up, her hair tangling around her shoulders, and he was facing eyes that held jarring anger. Her mouth was tightly set, her skin flushed, and her hands, holding a broken soup bowl, were shaking. "Fine, just fine," she muttered.

"Sir?" Hughes called to him.

E.J. had no idea why she was furious with him. It didn't make sense. He killed the impulse to ask her why she was looking at him like that, and when she turned to get back to the mess at her feet, he walked away. He followed Hughes to the bar area, sat on one of the leather-covered stools and ordered a black coffee. While the bartender got it, E.J. looked in the mirrors that backed the bar. He spotted the waitress coming across the space with the trayful of broken china and ruined food.

He assumed she'd go right past him and into the kitchen area, but he was wrong about that, too. She came right toward him, and as he turned, she faced him with just two feet separating them. He could almost feel her heat as he inhaled a combination of scents, from coffee to flowers.

Then she uttered in a low, tight voice, "What do you think you were doing back there?"

It was then he realized how attractive she was—her full bottom lip and her silky blond hair. The high color in her complexion only emphasized a delicate beauty that owed nothing to makeup. "Trying to help," he said truthfully, and found himself making an offer that shocked him. "Do you want me to have a talk with your boss about it?"

Now the color drained from her face. "Don't you dare! You've done enough." She looked back over her shoulder, then at him again. "Stay out of this. Please."

He remembered her flinching when the man had grabbed her arm, but he knew when to give up. "Hey, it's none of my business what you do or what that guy does to you."

The color was coming back into her face. "That's right, it isn't," she muttered, then turned and left him. He watched as the kitchen doors swung silently shut behind her. She was gone, and E.J. didn't have a clue as to why he'd gotten involved at all.

Life was crazy, and a waitress with aquamarine eyes was obviously part of that craziness today. He lifted his coffee and took a drink of the rich brew. He didn't need any more complications in his life, and if he was any judge of women, the waitress could be one huge complication.

CHAPTER TWO

SARA FLYNN STOPPED just inside the kitchen doors and was shaking so hard she had to put the tray down on the stainless steel counter before she dropped it. She tried to get her hair back in the knot, twisting it and pushing the pins to hold it, but she had a terrible time fastening it. As she pushed in the last pin, she took several deep breaths to try to steady herself.

"What's going on out there?"

She turned to the chef, Marv, who was doing prep work on a side table, chopping carrots and celery so quickly that the actions were almost a blur. "An accident," she said, and took the tray over to the sinks to dispose of the food and the broken dishes.

"Sounded like a bomb went off," he said.

"A bomb would have been preferable," she

said, dropping the tray into the soapy water in the large sink, then turning to Marv.

The chef was fifty or so, a stocky man with dark eyes and a ruddy complexion. She'd never seen him out of his whites. He'd been kind to her, explaining things she didn't know about the business, and covering for her when she'd needed it. He stopped chopping for a minute and frowned at her. "What was it?"

She shrugged. "I dropped that last order right on the customer," she said, trying to make her mouth smile, but it was impossible.

Marv smiled for both of them. "Oh, boy, I wish I'd seen it, although I hate to see my work ruined."

"You wouldn't have wanted to see it," she said. "Hughes is furious."

"Threatened to fire you, didn't he?"

She exhaled. "He sure did, and then some customer butted in, and…" She bit her lip, still remembering when she'd heard that deep voice and looked up to see the man standing over her. The way he'd reached out, taken Hughes by the arm—

and the anger behind his action. Dark hazel eyes hadn't backed down from Hughes and his fury, and she'd known if the stranger had said or done one more thing, Hughes would have fired her then and there to prove he could.

"A customer?" Marv said, cutting into her thoughts.

She looked through the small oval pane of glass in the kitchen door and saw the man. He was still at the bar, leaning forward, his elbows on the polished wood top, and staring into his coffee mug. "He's still at the bar. He said something about talking to Hughes about what happened, but I hope he's forgotten all about that." She watched the stranger sit back, turn and look at a man coming into the restaurant.

She recognized the security man from next door. He crossed to the man at the bar, said something, then left. The stranger turned back to the bar, tossed off the rest of his drink, then stood. He was tall and lean, and had an edge to him. A dangerous edge, she thought, then rationalized she was feeling that because he'd nearly gotten her fired.

"A real knight in shining armor?" Marv asked.

She turned as the man put a bill on the bar. "No. He almost got me fired." She ducked back when Hughes came toward the doors and stepped into the kitchen.

"Sara?" he said. "The tables aren't ready for the lunch rush. Get them set, then come into my office."

"Yes, sir," she said, her heart sinking. Quickly she went past him and out into the restaurant. Her luck was holding and all of it was bad. She barely missed walking right into the stranger, and she had the horrifying thought that he was following Hughes to have that talk with him.

"You," she muttered, stepping back to look up at him.

His eyes were a rich hazel, framed by fine lines and set under dark brows. Direct, cutting eyes that made her uncomfortable and angered Hughes. "Me," he murmured.

"What are you doing?" she asked, realizing that her whole body had tensed.

He studied her almost indolently for a long, nerve-racking moment, then tugged at the cuffs of his leather jacket. "I'm leaving."

"Good," she said with relief.

She regretted saying that as soon as the single word was out. He couldn't possibly know how precarious her life was at the moment, or how much this job meant to her. But before she could soften her words, he actually smiled at her. The expression made her tense again, but for a myriad of reasons. His eyes narrowed and something in them softened as his lips curved gently upward. The whole effect gave her a flash of something almost endearing, before it was gone and he murmured, "I'm not used to pleasing a pretty lady simply by getting lost. But I'm doing it now." He motioned to her hair. "Got some loose strands there," he murmured, then he turned and left.

She watched the door close and hated herself for being so cold to him. He was a stranger, someone she'd never see again, but if he ever happened to come into the restaurant when she was here, she'd make sure that she at least apologized.

"Sara. You're not on a break," Hughes said from behind her.

She headed for the side alcove. She reached for a basket with fresh linen napkins in it and started folding them into individual roses. She worked quickly, soon filling a tray with the soft roses, then went out into the dining area and started setting them out with the dinnerware on the tables.

All she wanted to do was get through this day, finish her lunch shift and go and pick up her daughter, Hayley, at the sitter's. They'd go back to the tiny house that was barely large enough for her and her three-year-old, and close the door on the world. It wasn't theirs, but it was home…for now.

Hughes called to her across the empty restaurant. "Sara, my office, now."

"Yes, sir," she said, and put down the last napkin.

She brushed her hands on her apron, then took a breath and headed for his office in the short hallway just off the rest rooms. When she stepped into the small space lined with boxes and filing cabinets and anchored by a large desk in the middle, Hughes was changing his soiled shirt. "Close the door."

She swung it shut, and when he didn't motion for her to sit, she stood with clasped hands and tried to head off a disaster. "Sir, I'm so sorry about the accident and it really won't happen again."

"Do you know who that man was you poured food on?" he asked as he pushed his arms into the shirtsleeves.

She'd seen him in the restaurant before, but she didn't know anything about him except he liked his coffee black and his salads dry. "No, sir."

He buttoned the shirt quickly. "For your information, Mr. Wise is one of the partners in the law firm of Broad, Simpson and Wise. One of the main tenants in this building, occupying two floors, six and seven…the entire floors."

She tried to pretend to be as impressed as he seemed to be. "I had no idea he was that important."

"All of our customers are important," he

said as he tucked in his shirt, then reached for his jacket from the back of his chair. "I just hope that I am able to make this right with him and his partners. But one more mistake like that and you are not going to be working here anymore."

If she could have handed him her job right then, she would have, but she didn't have that option. Since she and Hayley had moved to Houston two months ago, this was the only job she'd been able to find that had the right hours for her and gave her decent wages and tips. She was away from Hayley too much, but at least she had the second half of the day with her and she was there when she went to bed. "It won't happen again, sir."

He frowned at her as he retied his tie, and she knew he wasn't finished. "And you can tell that boyfriend of yours to keep out of your business. If he pulls something like that again, you'll both be out of here."

"My boyfriend?"

He tugged sharply at the cuffs of his jacket. "The man who so rudely interrupted us."

"Oh, he's not my boyfriend," she said quickly. "I don't even know who he is. I've never seen him before."

Hughes studied her, then smoothed his tie. "Just get back to work and remember that our customers expect excellent service."

"Absolutely," she agreed.

She went out of the office and returned to folding the napkins. The bartender, Leo, called out to her. "Hey, Sara?"

She turned. "What?"

"That guy who was just here? The one talking to you and Hughes over there?" He motioned to where the accident had happened.

Not him, too. "What about him?"

He held up two twenty-dollar bills. "He paid for his drink with these, then left. I hardly think he was so impressed with me that he left me more than a thirty-five-dollar tip. Can you tell him I've got his change whenever he wants to come and get it?"

"No, I don't know who he is."

"Oh, I thought you and he…" He shrugged and folded the bills, tucking them in his vest pocket. "I'll hold on to them and see if he comes back." The phone behind the bar rang, and as Leo answered it, Sara turned to go and check her drawer to make sure it was even before the lunch rush started. But she'd barely turned when Leo called out to her again. "Sara?"

She looked back at him. "What?"

He was holding the cordless phone out to her as he looked around. Then he whispered when she crossed to take the phone, "Hughes is gone. It's for you."

She felt her stomach sink. Only one person would be calling her—the baby-sitter. She took the phone and spoke quickly into it. "Marg?" she asked.

"Yes, hello, Sara. I'm sorry to be calling at work, but—"

"Marg, what happened? Is Hayley all right?" Her hand was holding the phone so tightly it was aching. "Is something wrong?"

"No, no, no, Hayley is just fine. She's napping right now, as a matter of fact. But I just found out something and wanted you to know right away." She hesitated, then said, "I won't be able to watch Hayley after this week."

Now her heart sank for a different reason. It had taken her forever to find someone to care for Hayley, someone she trusted and she felt safe leaving her child with. "For how long?"

"Actually, I'm going back to school. I've been thinking about it for some time, and the opportunity just came up. I can't pass it up," she said. "I'm sorry. I know this is an inconvenience for you, but I have a few recommendations for you, other sitters. I just wanted you to know right away."

"I appreciate that," she said, but thought it was more than an "inconvenience" for her. Another sitter? "I'll be by for Hayley later and you can give me the names?"

"Absolutely," Marg said brightly.

She hung up, then turned and handed the phone back to Leo. "Thanks."

"Your little girl okay?" he asked, surprising her by asking since she'd never spoken to him about Hayley.

"She's…she's fine," she said. It's just me, she wanted to add, but didn't. She wasn't going to wallow in self-pity. She hadn't been fired. Hayley was okay. Things would work out.

"Customer," Leo said, nodding toward the door.

For some reason she expected the stranger to be coming back, hoping it was, so that she could apologize. But when she turned there was no lean man in a leather jacket with a smile that seemed to see humor where none existed. Instead, she saw a lady whom she'd met the first day at work, Mary Garner, who helped run the day-care center in the LynTech building next door. Mary came in every day at this time to have a cup of tea and nibble on shortbread biscuits. The slender, gray-haired lady smiled when she spotted Sara.

"Hello, there," Mary said brightly.

The lady was in her sixties, with a gentle, soft voice. She wore simple dresses in grays or navies, and always sensible shoes. "Good morning," Sara said, and led her to her usual table, one off to the side by the windows. "The usual?" she asked as Mary settled into the high-backed leather chair.

"Yes, thanks," Mary said, then touched Sara's hand before she could leave to get the tea and biscuits. "Is everything all right? Your little one's okay, isn't she?"

Mary was the only customer Sara ever talked to for any length of time, and for some reason, she was the only person she'd told about her situation. "Hayley is just fine, thank you."

"Well, you look totally stressed," Mary murmured softly, then her eyes widened. "That husband of yours, he didn't show up here, did he?"

"Oh, no, it's nothing to do with Paul, and he's not my husband. We've been divorced for three months now, and as far as I know, he's off somewhere on the East Coast making musical history." She shook her head. "He's doing his own thing, and he won't think about us…not unless he needs money."

Mary sighed. "Then what's going on?"

"Just a bad morning," she said.

Mary tapped the table. "Can you sit for a minute?"

Sara was tired and the idea of sitting

down for a bit was very appealing, but she couldn't take a chance of making Hughes angry again. "I'd better not."

Mary looked past her, then lifted her hand. "Sir?"

Sara turned and realized that Mary was motioning to Mr. Hughes. She literally held her breath as he approached them. "Mrs. Garner? What a pleasure to see you here again," he said pleasantly in his clipped British accent. "I was just saying to our chef that you can set your watch by Mrs. Garner. Eleven o'clock, right on the mark." He glanced at Sara, then back at Mary with concern. "Is there a problem?"

"Oh, my goodness, no, sir. I just wanted to ask you if Sara could keep me company for a few minutes? I thought a few minutes of adult conversation before heading back to the children would be a treat for me."

She could tell by the way his jaw worked that he wanted to say no, to push Sara back into the kitchen to help with the prep work. But he nodded obsequiously. "For you, dear lady, anything." He looked at Sara. "Ten minutes?"

"Yes, sir."

He looked back at Mary. "Have a lovely day, Mrs. Garner."

"Thanks so much, Mr. Hughes," Mary said with a smile. "You are a prince among men."

He smiled at that. "And you are a true lady."

As he walked away, Mary patted the table across from her and said, "Sit down, dear."

"I'll get your tea first," Sara said, then hurried off and was back in a few minutes with a tray with two cups of tea and the plate of biscuits. She put them down in front of Mary, then slipped into the opposite seat.

She couldn't help glancing at Hughes over by the bar, and was shocked to hear Mary mutter, "Don't worry about that officious twit."

Sara looked at Mary. "He's my boss."

"A twit," Mary said, then took her time sipping tea, before she sat back in her seat. "Now, what's been happening?"

Sara fingered her teacup. "Well, to begin

with, I dumped a whole tray of food on one of the most important people in this building, according to Mr. Hughes."

Mary stared at her, then started to chuckle. "Oh, my."

"Exactly," Sara murmured, starting to smile in spite of herself. "He's a lawyer or something in this building, a Mr. Wise. You know the kind, a three-piece suit with polished fingernails."

Mary nodded. "Oh, yes, I do know that type."

"Then Hughes went ballistic," she said, picking up her cup. "He was livid, worried about me driving off customers. Then one of the customers stepped in, but I wish he hadn't." She had a sudden memory of those hazel eyes, and she clasped her hands around the teacup to steady them. "I was afraid Hughes was going to fire me on the spot."

"Well, he didn't, obviously."

"For now." She exhaled. "And my baby-sitter…" She shook her head. "Never mind. I hate people who have a laundry list of complaints if someone just says, 'How are you?'"

"I asked. But speaking of baby-sitters, I have an idea that I wanted to run past you if I could?"

Sara looked at her watch. "I've got a few more minutes."

"Okay, you know all about Just for Kids?"

"Sure, of course. It's a great idea for a day-care center, and I'm a bit surprised that a huge corporation like LynTech would let them set up over there."

"It started with LynTech," Mary said. "It was the brainchild of the CEO's wife, Lindsey Holden. But that's beside the point. Right now they're expanding, opening up to the public, bit by bit. That's where you come in."

"Oh, sure," Sara said with a wry smile. "I'm a whiz at business. I could give them financial advice."

Mary grinned. "You probably could, the way you manage to be a single parent to Hayley and work here and survive."

Sara laughed a bit ruefully. "That's about

all I do. Survive." She looked at the tea-cup and put it down. "By the way, I think we'll take you up on that movie offer this weekend."

"Wonderful! There's a little girl at the center, Victoria, she's four. I think I'll try to bring her with us." Mary had been widowed a couple of years ago and she'd never had children, according to the conversations they'd had. She'd said that was one of very few real regrets she had in life.

"I think a movie is a good idea," Sara murmured. It would be the first fun thing she'd done for Hayley since coming to Houston. Hayley needed some fun. And so did she.

"We'll plan on it for Sunday, and it's my treat." Before Sara could object, Mary said, "I have more than enough money, and I know you don't make a bundle working here. Let me treat, okay?"

Sara hesitated, then finally nodded. "Thank you."

"My pleasure," Mary said. "And speaking of money. Your sitter doesn't come cheap, does she?"

Marg had been more than she could afford, but not as bad as some she'd checked into. "She's reasonable," she said. "At least for now. She's closing business as of next week."

She didn't want Mary's sympathy, but she wasn't prepared for the woman to actually clap her hands and smile. "Perfect!"

"Excuse me?"

Mary's smile just grew. "You know, I truly believe in fate. That we meet others when we need to and things work out."

Sara didn't understand where that came from. "I don't see what—"

"It just so happens that they need someone to help out on a part-time basis at Just for Kids, someone good with children, and someone they can trust. You fill the bill. I think we could work out something where you could leave Hayley there while you work your shift here, then when you're done here, after lunch, you can come over there and spend the afternoon with her." Mary looked as pleased with herself as if she'd just figured out a way to bring about world peace. "It's perfect," she pronounced.

"It would be, but I can't afford something like that," she said.

Mary's smile didn't falter. "There's nothing to afford. That's the best thing about this plan. If you help us out for the afternoon, Hayley can be there all day for nothing. Now, you can't refuse an offer like that, can you? Still being able to work here while she's being looked after…and…you don't have to pay child care costs?"

She stared at the woman. "I'd work there?"

"You know how hard it is to get someone you can trust with children. And they're very particular about whom they hire over there. You've told me you worry about Hayley and who's with her. Well, you'd know who was with her and she'd be right next door."

Her tea was forgotten. "You think that I could do that?" she asked, not quite believing that she could be the recipient of this kind of good luck.

"Yes, I do. I talked to Mrs. Holden and she thought it sounded like a great plan."

"Oh, Mary, that…would be…it would be great," she managed to say around a lump in her throat.

"Sara!" Hughes came barreling out of the kitchen, striding in her direction like a man on a mission.

She stood quickly, picking up her teacup. "I need to get back to work."

"Tell you what, come in tomorrow right after you finish here, and we can all sit down and iron out the details and get you familiarized with the work involved."

"Thank you," she breathed just before Hughes got to them.

"Mrs. Garner, forgive me for the interruption," he said, then looked at Sara. "We just received a reservation for twenty in half an hour. We need to get things set up."

"Yes, sir," she said, and gathering her teacup, smiled at Mary. "Thanks, and I'll come by tomorrow," she said, then headed back to the kitchen.

"Sara?" Leo called to her.

She stopped by the bar. "What?"

"That guy, the one who left the huge tip?"

"What about him?"

"He left this, too," he said, and held up a single key.

She went closer and looked at the key, about three inches long, gold, with what looked like leather molded to the top of it and a monogrammed *E* on both sides. "What is it, a house key or a car key?"

"I don't know, but the guy is either locked out of his house, or his car's not going anywhere." He dropped the key in his tip glass, and said, "If he comes in again, and I'm not here, let him know?"

Apologize and get his key back to him if she ever saw him again. "Sure thing." But hopefully her mysterious defender wouldn't return. Otherwise she might lose this very necessary job for good.

CHAPTER THREE

One week later

IN THE MASTER suite of his ranch house just
south of Dallas, E.J. threw clothes into a
leather overnight case lying open on his
four-poster bed. The house, a sprawling
adobe structure that had once belonged to
the biggest oil baron in the area, was surrounded by rolling acres of grazing land.
He'd bought it because it let him be alone
whenever he wanted. He had the money to
do it, so why not. Although security was
breached from time to time, in general he
felt safe here.

At the moment, safety wasn't on his
mind. His father was. As he tossed in the
last of his clothes, he said, "Run that by
me again, Dad?"

He glanced over his shoulder at Ray
Dan Sommers, who stood, arms folded,

feet braced, without a bit of apology in his expression. Ray was sixty-five years old and looked every day of it, with weathered skin and a sinewy body that came from years of working the oil fields. And he'd just dropped a bomb on E.J. "You heard me, Sonny," his father said.

His father was sure he knew what was best for his only child, a thirty-nine-year-old whom he persisted in calling "Sonny" when he was trying to get something past him. E.J., dressed only in his jeans and boots, his dark brown hair still damp from the shower and slicked back from his now clean-shaven face, snapped his case shut. As he reached for a white T-shirt, he said, "Don't call me Sonny, and you heard me, too."

He tugged the shirt over his head, then pulled it down as he looked at Ray again. "Explain," he said tightly as he tucked the shirt into the waistband of his Levi's.

Ray backed up a bit as they met gazes, but he didn't back down. "It seemed like a real good idea. You know, it's PR, it's image-shaping, like the big boys say."

Ray was in his usual jeans, plaid shirt and worn boots. He frowned, drawing his gray eyebrows together over hazel eyes, and stroked the beard stubble on his chin. "With you back in negotiations with Lyn-Tech, it couldn't hurt for you to show your magnanimous side. Charity's good and it shows there's no hard feelings about that mess last week. Besides, it'll give you a big tax write-off to use your place in Houston for LynTech's charity ball." He shrugged. "It all works out."

"Why didn't you check with me first?" E.J. asked, his exasperation showing in his tone.

The son faced the father, each the echo of the other, but with twenty-five years of aging separating them. Ray almost matched his son's six-foot height, and they were both lean. Both had brown hair, Ray's laced with a good dose of gray.

"You're right, E.J., dead right," Ray conceded, catching E.J. a bit by surprise. His dad seldom backed down on anything. "You were busy with…" He shrugged.

"Well, you were with Heather, and you seemed busy."

"When was this?"

"A few days back. I came out, saw the two of you at the pool and figured you didn't need to talk business then."

Heather McCain had come out to see him before she left for New York. What Ray didn't know, and what was none of his business, was that they'd decided it was time to move on, that their relationship had run its course. He had a feeling she'd been waiting for some declaration of love, but it never came, so she'd cut her losses. "So you just agreed for me?"

"They were asking, and I didn't want to interrupt you about something like that, so I said it would be okay."

"Just let LynTech use my place in Houston for a charity ball for some day-care-center thing?" he asked, still annoyed but starting to think that it might not be a totally rotten idea. He didn't have much to do with kids, and probably never would, but it couldn't hurt to help out that way. He just hated being volunteered.

"They're doing stuff for a pediatric wing at the hospital, sort of sharing the donations or something, and the only place they had to hold it in was an old auditorium. That wasn't right."

"They use the place, and that's it?"

"Sure, mostly."

"Mostly?" E.J. shook his head with a sigh. "What else?"

"Nothing big. They just asked if you could be there for the ball. I said, sure you would."

"Dad, why on earth—"

"Why not? You can be there in a blink of an eye on that fancy helicopter you got waiting for you now. And you're going to be heading to Houston off and on during the year, now that the deal with LynTech is going through, and you agreed to stay involved for the first year. I just didn't know you'd be going up there before the ball and staying at the house."

"You were wrong," he muttered.

"Yeah, sure, I know. I thought you'd fly in, just zip there and zip back. Even so, the place in Houston is the size of a small country. You can have all the privacy you need, and you can do whatever you want. Invite Heather to visit if you want, and no one's the wiser."

He was right about the size of the sprawling estate in Houston. "Heather's in New York."

"Well, women always seem to find you irresistible," Ray said with a sly smile.

"They find my money irresistible," he muttered.

"Hey, you're my son, and the women find the Sommers men irresistible."

"Sure, Dad, sure," he said. But he knew one woman who didn't. The blond waitress with those aquamarine eyes. He remembered all too well her anger at him for trying to help, a memory that had sneaked back into his mind at the strangest times this past week. "I'm going for business," he said firmly as he turned and reached for his suitcase.

"And if Heather shows up there?"

"She's in New York and we aren't seeing each other anymore." He wished he hadn't said that last part when Ray came closer.

"Sonny? What did you do now? She was nice, real pretty, and you would have had great kids."

"Oh, Dad, I've told you, it wasn't serious. No marriage, no kids, nothing. And it's over."

Ray shook his head. "Sonny, you're almost forty. You should be thinking of settling down, thinking about my future."

He turned to his dad. "*Your* future?"

"Well, yes," he said with a gruff laugh. "You're my only kid, and I want to be a grandpa before I'm too old to enjoy it."

E.J. brushed that off quickly. "Don't even go down that road."

"You're quite a catch, Sonny. Even that fancy magazine listed you as one of the most eligible men in the state last year."

"Sure, and so was that singer with the shaved head and a lobster tattoo," he muttered.

"It was a scorpion," Ray said.

"Whatever."

"I'm glad you're doing this," his dad said.

He glanced back at Ray. "Doing what?"

"The deal with LynTech, you getting back on track with Ford after the fiasco of the leaks."

Ray hadn't given him any feedback when he told him he was thinking of scaling down his holdings or when he'd told him about the mess last week. "Why?"

"If you have less work to do, maybe you'll have more time to start looking around for someone to have those grand-kids with."

"What part of 'that's not going to happen' don't you understand?"

Ray frowned. "Never say never, Sonny. You've got a few months before you're forty."

E.J. laughed at that. "And you've got a few months before you're sixty-five."

"So?"

He crossed to the dressing room and disappeared inside to get his leather jacket, then came back into the bedroom. "So? Why don't you get married again? You're still quite a catch."

Ray shook his head. "Don't have no desire to do that. Your mother was the one woman who—"

"Could rope your heart," E.J. finished for him as he put his wallet in his pocket and crossed back to the bed to get his suitcase. "I know."

"She sure did," Ray said.

He'd heard that since he was five and his mother had died. That was it for Ray. There had been women now and then over the years, but as Ray said, "None worth bringing home." He faced Ray and nodded to the door. "I'm leaving."

"I'm walking you out."

The two men went together through the sprawling main house, their boot heels clicking in unison on the terra-cotta floors of the heavily beamed, adobe-walled rooms.

"You want me to come with you?" Ray asked as they crossed the great room, which was done in a southwestern decor and took up the center of the house and cut toward the back of the building.

"No, just take care of things here, and don't volunteer me for anything else."

"There was one other thing," Ray said as they got to the side exit, the one that led across a stone patio to a helicopter pad beyond a breadth of rolling lawn. "But it can wait."

E.J. didn't open the door, even though he could hear the throaty vibration of the helicopter ready to take him to Houston. He turned to look at his father. He didn't remember much about his mother, except her voice when she sang to music, but Ray had been the rock in his life. They'd been in the oil fields together, worked side by side, and when he'd "struck it rich," Ray had been there. But over the years, he'd learned to never let a casual "one other thing" pass unchallenged.

"Spill it," E.J. said.

"You gotta go, Sonny. You said you didn't want to be late for the meeting this morning."

"Don't call me Sonny," he said tightly. "And I'm not going until you tell me everything."

Ray shrugged. "I sort of told them you

might be able to get some of your friends to come to the ball."

E.J. rolled his eyes and sighed with ex-asperation. "Dad—"

"Don't worry about it," Ray said quickly. "I can make some calls and ask them to—"

"No," he said quickly.

"But they'll expect—"

"No! Just tell me that's it, that you didn't offer me for anything else."

"Just that you'll participate in a few things."

This was going from bad to worse. "Like what?"

"An auction they're going to have."

"And?"

"That's it. Everything."

"Nothing else?"

Ray spread both hands palms-up to his son. "I swear."

E.J. shook his head. "No more volun-teering me for anything. Got it?"

"Got it," Ray said.

"Okay, I'll be back in a few days. If anything comes up—" he paused, looking his dad right in the eye "—*anything, you call me.*"

"Absolutely," Ray said with a nod, then held out his hand. "Can you leave the key to the SUV? My truck's acting up and I need to do a few things while you're gone."

"Sure, but get the spare key from the drawer in my dressing room. I can't find the original anywhere."

"Okay. Have a good trip, Sonny," Ray said.

"That's the plan," he said as he opened the door and the throaty engine of the helicopter made the air around them vibrate. He hurried out onto the patio and jogged toward the waiting helicopter. He loved his dad, but he never knew what he'd get them into. Or get him into. This had turned out to be a rough deal, from leaks to miscommunication, and probably the decided perception the top brass at LynTech had about him. Truth be told, if Jackson Ford hadn't been there to talk him into reinstating the negotiations, this would have been over long ago.

He ducked low, climbed into the passenger seat of the helicopter and nodded to his pilot, Rick Barnes, who handed him a headset. He slipped it on and spoke into the mouthpiece. "Any word from Martin?" he asked Rick.

"He's in Houston already and will meet you at the car when you get there. He's got all the papers."

E.J. nodded, then, as the motor's rpms increased and the helicopter took off, he glanced back at the house. Ray was still there, lifting a hand toward him, and he waved back. Ray's assurance that there were no more surprises waiting for him in Houston hadn't rung true, but he hadn't had the time to dig. When he got back, he'd straighten everything out, including his dad.

SARA HURRIED INTO THE BACK of the restaurant, past Hughes's office and into the small room used for employee lockers. She quickly changed from her waitress uniform to jeans, a pink T-shirt and running shoes. "Wear something comfortable," Mary had told her last night when she'd called to check to make sure Sara would be bringing Hayley into the center before going to the restaurant for her shift. "Nothing good. Fingerpaint tends to find its way onto everything."

Sara had dropped Hayley off at the center before her shift, and was relieved when her daughter had been thrilled with the array of toys in the playroom, a wonderful climbing tree in the center of the space, with "tree houses" off in each corner. She'd squealed at a huge black-and-white pet rat in a fancy cage decorated with ribbons and with the plaque reading Charlie that hung over the door.

The three-year-old had barely spared Sara a hug when Sara had said she was leaving, but she'd be back. "She'll do just fine," Mary had said with a smile as Hayley ran off with a group of kids. "And we'll see you when your shift is done."

Sara had fought the urge to check on Hayley on her break, but now she was anxious to get over to the center. She tugged the pins out of her hair, freeing it from the knot, then she turned to the mirror by the stand of metal lockers. She was shocked to see she was actually smiling. It seemed forever since she'd smiled for no reason. She smoothed her hair, tugged the T-shirt down, then gathered her things, pushed them in her backpack and headed out of the room.

Ten minutes later, she was entering Just for Kids. At the moment it was a quiet space, with soft music playing through hidden speakers. In the main playroom, murals of children holding hands and laughing hung on the wall, and soft carpet covered the floor where the real children lay on colorful pads at the base of the huge, handmade, paper tree. Mary was sitting on the floor with her back against the trunk, her eyes closed. A large storybook lay open on her lap. Hayley was lying on her stomach on a bright pink pad, sleeping.

Mary must have sensed Sara's presence, because her eyes opened, then she held a finger to her lips. She got to her feet and smoothed her navy dress. "Nap time," she whispered, crossing to Sara and smiling. "We don't want to shorten it in any way.

Hayley just wore herself out, but she had a good time, I think."

Sara looked at her daughter, a tiny child for three, with blond hair, slightly flushed cheeks and dressed in pink overalls. "I bet she did."

Mary glanced at a helper Sara had met before, a sixteen-year-old girl, who wore black jeans and a black top with Whatever splashed in gold across the front. Even her hair was black and caught in two pigtails. She was helping at the center during her summer break from school, and was a daughter of one of LynTech's executives. "Mallory, keep an eye on things?" Mary asked in a hushed voice. The girl nodded and sat down where Mary had been.

"Come on into the office where we can talk," Mary whispered, then turned and led the way to the back of the room and down a short hallway. "We can talk in here," Mary said as she closed the door to Lindsey Holden's office and crossed to a desk that was overflowing with papers.

She sat down and motioned for Sara to do the same. "What a mess," she said, looking at the papers that littered the desk. "This charity ball is nothing but work," she said.

"It sounds very grand," Sara said. She'd heard all about the fund-raising event sponsored by the center through LynTech, to benefit the new pediatric wing at the hospital and the center itself. "And it should bring in a lot of money."

"Hopefully," Mary said with a sigh. "It's growing to gigantic proportions, though. The mayor will be there, a senator might show up. EJS Corporation offered the use of an estate on the outskirts of the city, and get this, the main house has an actual ballroom in it. We got very lucky and Marigold Events is donating their party-planning services for it. It's the premier party-planning company anywhere, from what I've heard, and Marigold Stewart herself is heading the staff."

"Marigold?"

"That's her real name, from what I can find out." She sat forward. "The reason I'm telling you all this is because we've been thinking that you could really be of use to all of us if you'd be a liaison of sorts between Marigold and the center."

"I thought I was going to be working here."

"Oh, you will be. All that means is, Marigold will contact you instead of me or Mrs. Holden, or Mrs. Gallagher, the other LynTech CEO's wife who also works at the Center. You might have to make a few trips out to the Sommers estate, maybe check out a few things, but other than that, you can do everything from here until the actual ball." She motioned to the office they were in. "Everyone uses this room, so you can, too."

She'd never planned more than Hayley's birthday parties, but she'd give it a shot. "Okay, just tell me what to do."

Mary pushed a stack of papers toward her. "Start here, and if you have any questions, holler."

Sara looked at the papers and saw floor plans and lists of everything from donations to attendees. The mayor was right at the top of it, and under it was E. J. Sommers. "This E. J. Sommers owns this place?"

"He sure does. And he'll be there. We have a promise of his appearance."

"He's important?" she asked.

"Important? Oh, I forgot, you're not from Texas. The man's a legend, dragged himself up by his bootstraps and made tons of money on some oil thing. He apparently does things his way and has fun doing it… Always has women after him."

"Let's hope he's not married," Sara muttered as bitterness rose in her throat.

"Oh, no, he's not married. He's been tied to Heather McCain, the daughter of a big political family in the state, for a while. You know the type, tall, pretty, rich? Maybe she'll bid on him at the ball."

"Bid on him?"

Mary leaned forward and tugged a sheet out of the stack. "A bachelor auction." She tapped the paper with her fingertip. "You know, pay for spending the evening with an eligible man? He's agreed to do it, and we're hoping he brings in a lot of money."

Sara picked up the paper and saw a minimum bid of two thousand dollars next to the man's name. "Well, I hope he's worth whatever he brings in," she said.

"From what I've heard, he is," Mary said with a grin.

"I HOPE THIS IS WORTH IT," Zane Holden, one of the two CEOs at LynTech, said as he sat forward and eyed E.J. on the far side of the huge conference table. "After all this work, it had better be everything Jack and Matt think it can be. We're here on good faith, all of us, and I hope that's the way you feel."

E.J. sat very still, waiting, knowing that whatever he said probably wouldn't fully satisfy Zane Holden. His mind was blurring from long hours of discussions that seemed to be going in circles. Between Ray's surprises and the hardball negotiations in this room, he was tired, but now he was back in the fray and in it for the duration. He had never been a patient man and he wanted this deal nailed down today or tomorrow.

Finally he said, "Of course, that's a given. We're all here on good faith."

Jackson Ford, sitting by Zane, had seemed vaguely distracted today, but even so, when he spoke, he hit the mark. "Okay," he said, his dark eyes narrowing as he ran his fingers through his deep-brown hair. "Let's just agree that we all want what's best and that we want this settled as quickly as possible. The figures are there. The rules haven't changed." He looked right at E.J. "The ball's in your court, so what are you going to do?"

Martin shifted in his seat next to E.J., but didn't say a thing. He wouldn't until he was asked to, even though E.J. knew he was itching to get in the middle of the fray. "I need a break," he said, and stood.

"Good idea," Zane said, and stood, too. The others started to get to their feet, and Rita, a woman who seemed to be the right arm to more than one of the executives at LynTech, closed her notebook and said, "Drinks are over there," motioning to a built-in bar by the windows.

As she turned to speak to Zane, E.J. saw

Martin head for the bar and pour himself a glass of water. E.J. flexed his shoulders, then left his paperwork on the polished conference table. He saw Ford say something quietly to Zane before he ducked out, then Robert Lewis, a spry-looking man, probably in his sixties, in a neat navy suit that was in direct contrast to his almost white hair, came around the table to where E.J was standing. Lewis, the founder of LynTech, was there as an adviser.

"I'm pleased that you showed up here today in person, instead of sending a hired hand." He glanced at Martin, who was by the bar talking to one of LynTech's accountants. "No offense to anyone, but it's always better to do business directly, rather than going through too many people."

E.J. looked back at Robert. "I'm glad you're here, too. You had the original vision for this company and I like the way you did business, being up front about everything."

Robert nodded. "In that vein, I'm interested in why you're selling off a piece of your company."

He liked this guy. No games, no oblique comments. Too bad Ray wasn't as straight-forward. "I'm doing it because I want to, sir. My life's too complicated and this will simplify it."

"An excellent reason," he murmured.

E.J. inclined his head slightly. "I thought so." He glanced around, then said, "I need to stretch my legs. I'll be back in…" He looked at his watch. "Half an hour."

Robert said, "Make it an hour. We all need a break."

E.J. nodded, then turned to find Martin next to him again. "We've got an hour."

"Good, we can go over—"

"No, I should have said, *I* have an hour. I need to get some fresh air and think."

"But, if you—"

"Martin, relax. I'll be back. Give me at least half an hour, then we'll talk before this gets back in gear."

Someone came up behind him and touched his shoulder. He turned to find a woman he hadn't seen before. She was a very delicate-looking blonde, very preg-nant and pale, but her smile was radiant. "Mr. Sommers. I'm Lindsey Holden. Zane's wife?"

"Yes, of course."

"I'm going home now, but I wanted to thank you so much for offering your estate for our ball. It was beyond generous, and it's greatly appreciated."

He felt a bit embarrassed by her effusive thanks. "No problem," he said, a real lie, but he wasn't going to tell her about Ray's manipulations. "I hope the event raises a lot of money."

"I'm sure it will," she said. "I heard you say you were going to take a break, and I was thinking, since you have a few minutes, why don't you go down to the center on the main floor and just take a look at it? The party planner is due in this morning, and you could talk to her or to Mary Garner."

That was the last thing he wanted to do, but he didn't have the heart to say that to her. "Maybe, if I have time."

She gave him a weak smile. "Good, good."

Zane was there, putting an arm around

his wife. "She'll talk your ear off about the center," he said with an indulgent smile. "But now she needs to get home and rest."

He nodded to E.J., then with his arm around his wife, Zane took Lindsey out of the conference room. Before anyone else could grab his attention, E.J. left, leaving his jacket in the room. He went out into the hallway, glanced in both directions, then started for the elevators. Once inside the car, he rode down to the main floor and intended to go directly outside and walk for a while.

But when the door opened, he saw a group of children coming into the building, maybe fifteen of them, chattering and laughing, with two women riding herd on them. He hesitated, then turned to his right, heading for a hallway that he hoped led to a rear exit and away from the kids. Despite what he'd told Lindsey Holden, he had no intention of being around kids during this break.

He found a back door marked Parking Garage, pushed it back and felt it hit something with a solid thud. He heard a gasp, the sound of things dropping, then he eased the door back cautiously. This time it swung open freely, and he was looking out at a girl in jeans and a pink T-shirt, going down on her knees on the cement floor. Blond hair fell around her shoulders, hiding her face, and pieces of colored paper, crumpled and stained with paint, seemed to be everywhere, spilling out of a torn green trash bag.

He hurried toward her, reached for her upper arm and tried to help her back to her feet. "Sorry. I didn't know anyone was out here."

Then she was on her feet, turning, pushing pale blond hair off her face with her free hand, and her aquamarine eyes met his as her husky voice uttered, "You?"

CHAPTER FOUR

THE MOMENT SEEMED to freeze in time. Him.
The stranger from the restaurant. Holding
her by the arm, not more than two feet
away, staring at her with as much surprise
in his hazel eyes as she knew was in hers.
"You?" she repeated, suddenly focused on
his hold on her arm. She turned, easing
out of the contact, and as he drew his hand
back, she could have sworn there was the
shadow of a smile playing at the corners
of his mouth.

"Me," he drawled.

She'd thought about seeing him again,
but it had always been a meeting in the restaurant, him coming in, her walking over
and very politely apologizing to him, then
telling him his key was in the tip jar. That
was as far as her imagination had taken
her. She'd never thought he'd knock her

down with a door, or that she'd be staring at him, tongue-tied. Nervous, she crouched and began to pick up the papers, trying to stuff them back into the ruined plastic sack, but they came out the torn side as quickly as she pushed them into the bag.

The next thing she knew, there was a metal clang on the cement, and she glanced to her right to see the stranger's denim-clad legs and scuffed cowboy boots right beside her, along with a stainless steel trash bin.

"Try this," he said as he hunkered down beside her and reached for the papers.

"Thanks," she muttered, catching a glimpse of his hands, large, strong-looking hands, without any rings. Working hands, she thought, with plain, square nails, not like those of that man at the restaurant whom she was sure had been wearing clear nail polish. "Let me do that," he said as he took the papers out of her hands, gathered up the last of them and pushed them into the container.

As they both stood, she took stock of him. Now he wasn't wearing a leather jacket. He was in a plain white T-shirt that clung to broad shoulders and a strong chest, along with plain jeans and scuffed leather western boots. He dressed like a lot of men she'd seen around Houston, yet was unlike anyone she'd ever met. He had that way of looking at her, with narrowed eyes that made her nervous. He tucked the tips of his fingers in his jeans, snugging the denim on his narrow hips, and inclined his head.

"Are you okay?" he asked in a low voice.

She felt heat in her face and lowered her gaze. But she regretted that as soon as she realized that his jeans were as snug as his T-shirt. She looked up right away, met his slight smile and prayed that he didn't notice her blush. "I'm fine, and I…I'm glad we ran into each other again," she said.

"Oh, you are, are you?" he asked.

She shifted from foot to foot, feeling like a child standing in front of a parent trying to apologize for something. "I meant that I wanted to say how sorry I am for acting the way I did before, for what I said and everything. I know you were just trying to help and I…" She bit her lip hard. "I shouldn't have reacted the way I did."

"Why did you?" he asked bluntly.

She shrugged, meeting his gaze evenly. "Should I have fallen at your feet and kissed your boots?" she asked with a touch of sarcasm that she really hadn't intended.

All he did was grin at her again. "Now, that has definite possibilities."

She felt her face flame. "Sorry. That was…"

"Uncalled for?" he provided.

"Yes, and if you must know, I was afraid that Hughes would fire me on the spot, and I can't afford to be out of work."

"Why didn't you just say that?" he asked.

She shrugged. "I never thought of explaining myself, and I was afraid if you said any more that he'd get angrier and—"

"He'd get rid of you?"

"Exactly," she said.

"Did he?"

"No, he didn't. He gave me another chance."

"How magnanimous of him," he murmured.

"He's the boss," she countered. "He might be an officious twit, but he's my boss."

That brought a rough chuckle. "Officious twit? I've met the type," he said.

"Then you know what I'm up against."

"Yes, I do. And I'm glad that you still have a job. But does that job mean you do janitorial work over here?"

She tucked her hair behind her ears. "No, this is another job."

"Two of them?" he asked with a lifted eyebrow.

"At the moment," she said.

"Do you have plans for more?"

"You never know," she sighed, and wondered why she was saying anything to him beyond the apology. "I should be getting back. I just wanted to apologize for the way I acted last week."

"Apology accepted," he murmured.

"Do you work here?"

"Excuse me?" he said.

"You're here. I assumed that you work here, too?"

"You said you work here, didn't you?"

he asked, answering her question with a question.

"I just started at the day-care center."

"That's a coincidence," he said.

"You work at the day-care center?" she asked, finding it hard to envision him around the gang of kids she'd just left inside.

"Me? No," he said, as if she'd asked him to jump out of an airplane without a parachute.

She actually found herself laughing. "You look horrified. Kids scare you?"

"Scare me? No. But I can't say that I have any affinity for them."

"You don't have any children, I take it?"

"No," he said, in exactly the same tone he'd assured her that he didn't work at the center.

"They do scare you, don't they?" she asked.

"No, but I don't have—"

"Any affinity for them?" she supplied.

He chuckled again. "You've got it."

"Okay, if you don't work at the center, what do you do?"

"Work. Long hours."

"Here?" she asked.

"At the moment," he said.

She had the feeling that getting answers would be a time-consuming task. "Janitor?"

"What?"

"Are you a janitor? You knew where the trash receptacle was."

"I looked up and it was there," he said.

She studied him. "Are you in security?"

"No," he said with a slight smile.

"Oh, you're a secretary?"

That brought a burst of laughter that echoed in the cavernous space, the humor going all the way to his eyes. "Me? No way."

"Sexist, aren't you."

"Not so I ever noticed," he said, but the smile was still there.

"You aren't going to help me on this, are you?"

"On what?"

"Finding out why you came out of that door and knocked me on my…" She felt heat in her face again, and cursed the way she could blush for no reason. "Knocked me over."

"I was coming out to get some fresh air."

"In here?"

"A drove of kids was coming in the front door, so I did the sensible thing and went in the opposite direction. That meant coming out here, which, I'm assuming, if it's like most parking garages, has an exit to the outside."

"I'm sure it does. This is my first day at the center, so I'm not very well versed on LynTech."

"Since you're from the day-care center, I guess it's a good thing I ran into you... so to speak." That grin was there again. "I came for fresh air, then I was told to go into the center and see someone about the charity ball."

That's what he was here for? He was working on the ball? "Well, this is really a coincidence," she said. "I'm the official liaison for the ball plans."

"So, you know everything about this ball?"

"No, but I can find out anything. Mary

Garner, the woman I work for, has been filling me in on it."

"Then you know where it's being held?"

"Oh, yes, but I still can't believe that there's a house around here that has its own ballroom, can you?"

"I never thought much about it," he said.

"From what I heard, it's part of the conspicuous consumption of the oil boom. You know, the old 'I can make my house bigger than yours' mind-set?" She'd heard about that time, the crazy money spilling all over the place. "Have you seen the house?"

"I've been there."

"Then you've met E. J. Sommers?"

"I've seen him."

"Well, I must be out of the loop, because I've never even heard of the man until today. Everyone else seems to be in a tizzy about him."

"Tizzy?" he asked, looking a bit taken aback at her words.

"You know, all excited and starstruck?"

He exhaled roughly, almost dismissively. "Starstruck? He's a businessman now, and was a wildcatter on the oil fields before that. Hardly a star."

"Well, you wouldn't know it by the way they talk about him."

"Oh?"

"It seems that he's a whiz at business. Everything he touches turns to gold. Although there seems to be a consensus that he's succeeding because he's got more luck than business savvy. That he's a bit of a playboy, lots of pretty women, but he's sort of going with Heather McCain now. Money attracts money, I guess." She wouldn't tell him that even Mallory, one of the day-care workers, had said, "He's so gorgeous and he's got this wild edge to him, as if you'll never know what he'll do next." Instead she said, "And he sort of thumbs his nose at convention."

"He sounds like a total reprobate," he murmured.

She shrugged. "I guess it's all a point of view. But even if he is a reprobate, it's a nice thing for him to offer his place for the ball. He must care about kids." She met his gaze. "I guess he has an affinity for children."

"Or maybe an affinity for tax write-offs," he said with a touch of grating sarcasm that seemed to come from nowhere.

"That's cold," she murmured. "You should give him the benefit of the doubt, no matter what he has an affinity for."

"Oh, you're the kind of person who only sees the good in people, aren't you?"

That jarred Sara, because she had been like that, a very long time ago. It had all but ruined her life. She'd only seen the good in Paul, even when others told her what he was. She hadn't seen the truth in him until it was too late, until they were married and had a child and all her dreams had been put on hold. The man she'd thought he was hadn't existed except in her mind. "No. You have to be realistic. But that doesn't change the fact that it's good that the man offered the mansion for the ball. On the other hand, I'm glad that I don't have to have anything to do with him."

"Point taken," he murmured.

"I just meant that I wouldn't expect a man like that to have any business with me."

"You're probably right. He's got things to do, places to go, people to meet," he said.

"Exactly." She frowned. "You never told me who I apologized to."

"What?"

"You never told me your name."

"Neither did you," he countered.

She hesitated, then held out her hand. "Sara Flynn."

He took her hand in his, engulfing her with heat, strength and a firm grip. "Nice to meet you, Sara Flynn."

He held her hand for a long moment, until she started to feel uncomfortable again. But she fought the urge to pull free. "Your name?" she said.

He hesitated for a second before he said simply, "Edward."

"That's it?" she asked.

He narrowed his eyes. "Edward's a respectable name, isn't it?"

She drew back then, feeling heat in her

face again. "Of course it is. It probably means something great, too."

He shrugged. "I don't have a clue what it means."

And E.J. didn't have a clue why he didn't tell her who he was right then and there. What did it matter? She thought E. J. Sommers was a rich jerk. And she didn't know who he was. He had a feeling if she knew, she'd run in the opposite direction. She'd get that look, either of avarice or disgust, and he didn't want to see either in those eyes. Despite everything, he wanted to keep this going for a while longer. It was refreshing to talk to someone who didn't measure every word, or just agree because of who they thought he was.

"You can look it up."

"Look up what?" he asked, losing track of their conversation for a moment.

"The meaning of your name. There are books and books on names."

"I'll look it up," he murmured.

"You said you came down to talk to someone about the ball, and that someone is me."

He was never at a loss for words, but for the life of him he couldn't figure out what to say without giving away who he was and why he was here. "The ball," he repeated. "Yes, the ball. The big fancy party."

"That's the one," she said with a smile that touched her amazing eyes and softened her full lips, lips that were intriguingly seductive and had been from the first moment he'd seen her.

"Sure, yes, of course," he heard himself stammering like some high school kid with raging hormones. "I needed to know…um…" He drew a thought out of thin air. "Is there insurance in case there is damage done to the Sommers estate?"

She stared at him, then shook her head. "Well, you sure had me fooled." For a moment his heart sank as her eyes flicked over his jeans and T-shirt. "I thought all you legal types wore three-piece suits and polished your fingernails, like that man I dumped the tray on last week. But here you are, dressed like that, and working in Legal. Who would have thought it?" Relief swept through him.

"I haven't conformed to too much of anything in my life," he found himself saying with real truth.

"But legal things conform to the letter of the law."

"You got me on that," he said. "Speaking of that, how about the insurance?"

"I'll have to find out and get back to you," she said. "Give me your extension and I'll call when I find out?"

That wouldn't work at all. "I'll be tied up all afternoon, so why don't I get back to you?"

"Sure, okay."

"What time do you get off work here?"

"I'm staying until six to take care of the late pickups."

"Okay, tell you what. I'll come down at six and find you."

She nodded. "Okay, six it is."

"Six it is," he whispered as he watched her walk away, wondering what he'd just done.

As six o'clock neared, E.J. was sure that Zane Holden and Matt Terrell should have sent Sara Flynn a thank-you card for the deal he agreed to with them. If he hadn't been thinking about seeing her again, he might have fought a few points of the negotiations and not made some concessions to get on with things and guarantee that he wouldn't be there far into the night. But in the larger scheme of things, he'd just wanted to get the deal solidified and ready to be drawn up for signing tomorrow, so he could get out of there on time. At 5:50, he left the conference room with the promise to be there at ten in the morning.

"Good job," Martin finally said as their elevator car approached the ground floor. "Not great, but good."

"I'll settle for good," E.J. said as the elevator stopped. "You take the car to the house. Security will let you in and give you the new codes. Make yourself comfortable in the west wing, and I'll be back…when I get back."

Martin hesitated as the doors slid open. "Is there a problem?"

"No," he said, glancing to his right as he stepped out of the elevators. He saw two doors in primary colors with a decal of children joining hands and dancing under the words JUST FOR KIDS, printed in block letters directly across from them. "I have something I need to do."

Martin smiled knowingly as he stopped, facing him. "Oh, I get it. Okay, okay, no questions. I won't even ask if it's Heather or someone else."

"For what it's worth, Heather isn't in the picture any longer," E.J. said. "And I need some cash for a cab."

Martin shook his head as he took out his wallet and handed E.J. several folded bills. While E.J. pushed them into the pocket of his leather jacket, Martin said, "I'll see you when I see you?"

"That works for me," E.J. said.

Martin nodded, then he headed off toward the front entry.

E.J. didn't cross to the doors of the center. If he walked in the front, chances were he'd run into someone who recognized him. Whatever was going on with Sara would be over before it began. He wasn't sure what was going on exactly, but he knew that he wanted to find out. He turned and went back the way he'd gone earlier in the day, heading for the back exit. This time he eased the door open slowly, then stepped out into the almost empty parking garage.

He looked around, then headed over to the door he'd watched Sara go through earlier. He reached for the handle, but it didn't move. It was locked. Maybe he'd have to take a chance and go through the main entrance if he wanted to see Sara, but just when he'd decided to turn around, the door suddenly swung outward.

He stepped back quickly, then turned and she was there. Sara stood in the entry, grinning at him mischievously. For that moment, she looked like a teenager who was very pleased with herself. "I thought I heard someone out here. Almost got you, didn't I?" she asked.

He smiled back at her. "Pretty close."

"I'll practice, " she said. "Come on in."

"Who's here?" he asked before he went inside.

"Just me. Everyone else has gone, at

least for now, and I have the insurance information."

He'd forgotten about the insurance ploy he'd used, but followed her inside and down a wide hallway. He watched her ahead of him, the way she moved, the swing of her hair as it brushed her shoulders and the soft swelling of her hips. No, she wasn't a teenager, he thought, and inhaled that flowery scent that seemed to cling to her. She stopped and turned, touching her forefinger to her lips. "I'll get the papers," she said in a whisper, and motioned to an open door to her right.

He didn't understand the whisper until she went through the open door and he went far enough to glance into a square room furnished like an office, except for a sleeping mat in the corner. A tiny girl was curled up on the mat, sound asleep. Sara glanced at her, then back at him. "We'll talk outside, okay?"

"Sure," he said, watching the little girl with blond hair shift, stretch a tiny arm over her head, then settle with a sigh.

He backed into the hallway, then Sara

was there with a folder in her hands. She took a quick look back into the office at the child, probably one of the kids waiting for their parent to show up to take them home. Then she led the way into a huge room that looked like something out of a child's stage play. A stylized tree in the middle branched out to all sides, and murals covered the walls. Toys were everywhere, but with a semblance of order, stacked in colorful crates and lined up on long, low shelves. Sara crossed to a cluster of tiny tables that looked like mushrooms, ringed with brightly colored miniature stools, and put the folder on the closest table.

She pushed the stools away, then dropped down on the carpet at the table cross-legged. She looked up at E.J. "Sorry, this is the best I can do with the office taken up."

He sank down on the carpet across the table from her, feeling like Gulliver in Lilliput. "So, you found out about the insurance?"

She pointed to the folder. "It's all in there, but Mary said that she sent all of the information up to Legal last week."

He'd never been good at lying. "Double-checking, that's all," he murmured, hoping that would cover the lie enough to keep it going for a bit longer.

She nodded, as if he'd said something rational. "Sure, attorneys need everything checked and double-checked."

"You sound as if you know attorneys," he said, for something to say.

She exhaled. "No, not really, but…" She bit her lip.

"But, what?" he asked.

She waved a hand as if what she was going to say was inconsequential. "At one time, long ago, I was going to go to law school." She smiled, a slightly off-kilter expression that seemed half joking and half apologetic. "Pie-in-the-sky notions, as my mother used to say."

"Why? You seem bright enough, and although I'm not sure the world needs more lawyers, why shouldn't you do it?"

The smile was gone now, and he could tell that something she'd try to pass off lightly actually meant a great deal to her. Or it had. "Life changes, we change, and maybe the time for a dream passes," she said, then laughed, but it was almost nervous now. "And I don't have a clue why I'm telling you all of this. After all, I hardly know you. I mean, I know your first name, Edward, or is that your last name?"

"First. Edward."

"That's it? Just one name?"

"Jonathan."

"Jonathan. Edward Jonathan." She said his first and middle name, as if testing them on her tongue. "Nice," she said.

He realized he was staring at her mouth and made himself stop. He pressed his hands flat on his denim-clad thighs. "So, you gave up the law and became a waitress?"

His words brought a bit of a smile back to her lips. "That wasn't planned, but I'm going to go back to college…some day, and take up where I left off before…" Her voice trailed off.

"Before what?"

"Before life got in the way," she said with a sigh. "Do you need me to make a copy of the papers for you?"

He was tired of the ruse and just wanted to talk to her. "No, I can take a look here, just to say I saw it," he said, and reached for the folder.

"Okay, you read the papers and I'll be right back," she said, getting to her feet in one motion and walking past him toward the back of the center.

He took the folder off the mushroom table and flipped it open because it was there. He read a policy for insurance, enough to take care of the expenses if a disaster occurred at the event, and added insurance in the event that the ball had to be canceled for any reason. Someone had done a thorough job on the insurance aspects of the ball. A good job. He put the folder back on the table and pushed up to his feet.

He took a breath, then suddenly *felt* Sara behind him. He wasn't sure if he'd heard her come back into the room or not, but he could quite literally feel her there without looking. A memory came to him, when he'd been maybe five years old, just after his mother had died. Ray and he had been sitting on the porch of an old house they'd rented. Ray had been drinking a bit more than he should have when out of the blue he said, "You know, Sonny, when I met your mama, I knew."

"Knew, what?" he'd asked.

"I felt her when I couldn't even see her there. I felt her and I knew."

E.J. hadn't understood what he'd been trying to say, not until right now. He knew now that Ray had been referring to that awareness of another human being, "knowing" she was there without even having to see her. But he'd just met Sara. They'd only talked for a few minutes. He hardly knew her. But when he felt her coming back into the room, and he turned to see if he was crazy, E.J. was all too aware of this beautiful woman.

CHAPTER FIVE

E.J. WASN'T CRAZY.

Sara was there, carrying the little girl he'd seen in the office. She cuddled the child into her, with her huge blue eyes wide open now and staring at him. "Hayley," she was saying as they both came closer. "This is Edward."

The little girl watched him closely, her cheeks flushed from sleep and her pale hair tousled. Sara stopped in front of him and that feeling of awareness was wreaking havoc with him. It shouldn't be like this, seeing her, only touching her once but realizing that he wanted nothing more than to kiss her. "Hayley?"

"Hayley, this man is Edward."

The child twisted away from Sara slightly to get a better look at him. "Edwood," she said in a tiny voice, making his name sound as if it had no *R* in it.

"That's me," he said, and wished that her parents would come and get her so he could do what he had wanted to do since he'd agreed to meet Sara here at six. He had planned to ask her out to dinner. That would give him time to tell her who he was and just plain get to know her.

"Were the papers okay?" Sara asked, patting the child softly.

"A good job, actually. Great coverage."

"Oh, good. Mary will be happy to hear that. She's stressing over everything, including the crazy idea that Mr. Sommers could just cancel his offer."

"That's not going to happen," E.J. said.

"Oh, so you're psychic now?" she asked, letting the little girl get down when she started to squirm in her arms. Hayley ran over to the shelves and dug into a basket.

"Don't you think it would be lousy public relations to do something like that?"

"Lousy," she agreed.

"But I wish I was psychic," he said.

She wasn't looking at him now, but

watching Hayley, who was gleefully tossing small blocks at the wall. "No throwing, Hayley." Remarkably the child stopped and began to stack blocks in a precarious tower pattern. "Good girl." Then Sara looked back at E.J. "I'm sorry, what did you say?"

"I was saying that I—"

"Mommy! Mommy!" Hayley called as she turned and ran toward them. "Look, look!" she was saying, holding out something in her hand.

E.J. turned, expecting to see the child's mother coming into the center, but there was no one there. When he turned back, Sara was crouching in front of Hayley, taking what looked like a headless plastic doll from her. "She's boke," Hayley said. "Boke, fix it."

Sara laughed softly. "Sorry, honey, but Mommy can't fix her. It seems she's lost her head."

Mommy? E.J. stared at the two of them, realizing now that Hayley was a tiny version of Sara. Blond, delicate.

A child? "She's yours?" he asked before he could think of editing his words.

Sara stood with the doll in her hands, her aquamarine eyes meeting his gaze. "All mine."

And that was that. "Married with children" ran through his mind, but all E.J. said was "Oh." It didn't matter what he felt or thought he felt, she was off limits. Whatever he'd wanted to say earlier, the dinner he was going to take her to, was no longer an option.

Sara frowned slightly at him. "You were saying something before Hayley started her target practice with the blocks?"

"Nothing." He reached down for the folder and handed it to her. "Thanks again. You must be in a hurry to get home."

"It's been a long day," she said with a sigh, her eyes going to the child, who had discarded the headless doll in favor of the blocks again. "But I have to wait for Mary. She's supposed to come back and give me a ride." She looked at E.J. "I didn't bring my car today. She wanted to pick me up, to get me started right, as she said, but she had to take care of some business." She glanced at the wall clock. "She said she'd be back by six-fifteen."

He looked at the clock himself. "She's late."

"She's busy," she said, and looked at Hayley again. "As long as Hayley's happy playing, I'm okay."

He knew he should thank her and leave. That he should wish her a good evening and walk out the door. But instead he found himself saying, "How about your husband? Maybe he could come and get you?"

She turned to him, her eyes narrowing slightly, and he definitely could see her lips tighten. "No, he can't," she said in a low voice.

She's a widow, he thought, and felt his throat tighten. "Oh, I'm sorry." The words came automatically, just as automatically as some deep impulse to touch her, the same impulse that made him push his hands into his jacket pockets.

She was very still, then her eyes widened slightly. "Don't be. He's not dead," she said. "We're divorced."

Divorced? If there wasn't the child in the mix, he might have felt real relief to find out she wasn't married. He might have. "Oh," he said again, at a loss for words.

"We'll wait for Mary," Sara said.

"You will, will you?"

E.J. heard a third party speaking, and Sara turned toward the entrance and smiled. He saw an older woman hurrying into the center, coming toward them, but when she saw him, she hesitated just a fraction of a second. Her eyes narrowed and her head inclined slightly to one side as she came closer. He could almost hear her thinking, "Is that E. J. Sommers?" It didn't matter now.

"Mary," Sara said, and E.J. heard the child scrambling, blocks going everywhere, then she was there, cutting between her mother and Mary.

"Mawy, Mawy," Hayley said, holding up her arms to the older woman.

Mary picked her up in one easy motion. "Hi, there, sweetheart," she murmured, her gaze back on E.J.

"Mary, this is Edward from Legal, the man I told you about earlier?" Sara said.

Mary let Hayley wiggle out of her arms and put her down, then held her hand out to E.J. "Edward," she said with just the slightest hint of question in the name.

He took her offered hand, waiting for her to say something. "Mary," he murmured, inclining his head to her.

"So, is Legal satisfied?" she asked him evenly.

Maybe he'd misread her, and she didn't have a clue who he was. Maybe he was hypersensitive because of a guilty conscience. "As far as I can tell, the policy covers everything."

"Well, that's good to hear," she said. "I thought Legal was satisfied before, since they were the group that put the policy together." She inclined her head slightly. "A contribution from LynTech, getting us the insurance."

"Sure, but you can never be too careful checking things out," he said.

"Well, that's true," she said. "Very true." Then she looked at Sara. "I'm sorry for being so long, dear," she said. "And now it seems that I'm going to have to work here a bit longer. I know you had your early shift at the restaurant, and it's been a long day for you, I just wish I hadn't talked you into letting me drive you in today."

"Oh, don't worry about it. Hayley and I can hang out here. That's not a problem."

"Oh, dear," Mary said with a shake of her head. "You were here so early, and now it's getting late, and you have to be at the restaurant early tomorrow." She looked at E.J., silently asking him to step in. He didn't. He'd hit a brick wall with Sara and he was ready to walk away. He had no intentions of getting involved with any woman who had children.

When he didn't speak up, Mary looked back at Sara. "Well, I guess you could take my car and I could take a taxi, or...something?"

The woman was the perfect passive-aggressive type. Make him feel like a fool for not offering Sara and the kid a ride, and he'd do it? He looked at Mary, met her gaze, and he knew he was right.

"Unless...?" Mary was honing her skills quickly. "Edward, do you have a car here?"

He looked right at her. "No."

"You're walking?"

It was getting to be a game with her. "No."

He felt Sara staring at him and didn't dare look at her. One look into those aquamarine eyes and who knew what he'd succumb to? "Flying?" she asked, her mouth twitching with the shadow of a smile.

"Not this time," he murmured, then made a fatal move. He looked away from Mary and at Sara. What a huge mistake. "I'm calling for a taxi," he admitted, as if he'd gone through significant torture, then had endured one last twist before he spilled his guts. "Do you want to share a cab?" he asked, feeling like a broken man.

Had he expected Mary to cheer and Sara to thank him profusely for the offer? If he had, he was wrong. Mary didn't say anything, and Sara spoke up immediately. "Oh, no, thanks, we'll wait."

He had his out. He could leave. He had

some honor, at least he thought he did. "Okay, I need to get going."

But Mary wasn't done. "Sara, honey, that's a perfect solution." She reached in her purse and took out a ten-dollar bill, offering it to Sara. "Let the center treat you for your first day?"

Sara shook her head. "No, I couldn't."

Stubborn? Proud? Maybe. Then again, maybe she just didn't want to be with him any longer than she needed to. Maybe he wasn't the only one looking for a way out of this. "Whatever you say," he said.

"I might be here until...ten or so," Mary said quickly.

Sara didn't want to do this. She didn't want to be with Edward any longer. It was too easy to look at him, meet his expression and start smiling like a starstruck teenager. She didn't want to have so much awareness of anyone. "Been there, done that," she thought. "Mary, I can't just—"

"Just what, dear?" Mary asked earnestly, as if she really wanted to understand why Sara was refusing a perfectly good offer from an attorney at LynTech.

She was too tired and couldn't come up with anything that wouldn't sound rude, so she said half of the truth. "I can't afford a taxi."

Mary still had the ten-dollar bill in her hand and held it out to Sara again. "Take this."

Sara could feel that Edward didn't want to do this, either, but she was out of arguments. She took the bill, crumpled it in her hand. "Thanks."

Then she made herself look at Edward, hoping he'd come up with some reason why they couldn't share a cab, but all he said when she met his gaze was "Are you ready to leave?"

"I need to get a few things from the office," she said, and hurried away. Just a trip home. That was it, she told herself as she grabbed her backpack, pushed her purse in it and reached for the car seat. She stopped in the middle of the office when she realized that her heart was hammering against her ribs and she felt flushed.

She forced herself to take several deep breaths, to get some semblance of control before she went back out into the play area. She wasn't going to her doom, just taking a ride with a man. She headed back, and she found Edward and Mary talking in low voices. She watched Hayley toss blocks into a box, then said to Mary and Edward, "Okay, I think I'm ready."

They both looked a bit startled when she spoke, then Mary recovered and smiled at her. "I was just talking to Edward about the ball."

Edward came toward her, taking the car seat and backpack out of her hands. "I called for a cab and it should be here by the time we get out to the entrance."

Sara went to get Hayley, picking her up, then shifting her to her hip. "I'll see you in the morning," she said to Mary.

"I'll be by to pick you up," she said.

"No, thanks, I'll drive myself," she said, not about to get into this situation again. "I'll meet you here first thing."

"Okay, dear," Mary said, then glanced at Edward. "Thank you."

He started for the entrance and Sara followed. Edward stopped by the glass doors of the building, told her to stay inside until he made sure the taxi was coming, then he went out and spoke to the security man.

When he was through, E.J. looked at Sara with Hayley through the glass door and knew if it wasn't rude, he would have let her take the taxi and leave. She stirred up too many ideas. But seeing her with the child on her hip, he knew he couldn't do that. He opened the door, shifting the car seat and backpack in his arms. "The taxi should be here any minute," he said.

Without warning, she gave him his out. "Thanks for helping, but I can go alone from here," she said.

He looked back at her with the seat in his hand. "What?"

She was looking right at him, softly patting the little girl's back. "I can take it from here, if you'll just help me get the car seat into the cab."

It was then he knew he wasn't going to leave her to "take it from here." "I said I'd go with you, and I will."

"You don't want to, so why are you?" she asked bluntly.

He hadn't thought he was that transparent. "I said I would."

"You only came down for the insurance information, and you have that. So, your work is done, no matter what Mary manipulated us both into."

The truth was there. "No, you're not right about that," he said.

Her eyes narrowed and the child looked at him, too. She had the same expressions as her mother. "You asked for the insurance information, and—"

"Yes, I did, but I also had this idea that if I came down, and you were there…" He shrugged. "I was going to ask you to dinner," he admitted bluntly.

Her eyes widened slightly. "Oh," she said, then shifted the child to her other hip and smoothed the little girl's pale hair. "Then I guess you've changed your mind?"

He'd gone this far, so he decided to be truthful. "I didn't know about her," he said, nodding to Hayley.

She exhaled. "And you have no affinity for children?" she said in a low voice, but without any anger in it.

Now he felt like a selfish jerk. "I just never get involved with—"

"A woman with children," she said, a statement, not a question. "You have your priorities straight, and that's okay." She jarred him by smiling, but in a way that didn't reach her eyes. "I have mine straight, too. I wouldn't have gone out to dinner with you, anyway, so don't look so bothered."

Now, that stung, and he wasn't about to let it pass. "That's a relief," he lied. "But why wouldn't you have?"

"Because I don't date, and Hayley is my priority, period."

He didn't know when he'd lost control of everything, but he had...completely. "So, you're sacrificing yourself for your child?" he heard himself say, and he hated the tinge of sarcasm in the question.

Color stained her cheeks and she looked away, down at her daughter in her arms. "I'm her mother. It's not a sacrifice."

"And mothers don't date?"

She looked at him, her expression tight. "Most mothers are married," she said.

"Why aren't you still married?" he heard himself ask, and wondered why he even wanted to know why she walked out on her husband and the child's father.

"My husband...my ex-husband, he didn't want to be married," she said, and he wished he'd never asked. Then he wouldn't have seen the pain in her eyes, despite the even way she responded. "It's just me and Hayley."

"And you'll never date?"

She shrugged. "I don't know. If there was someone who could love Hayley as much as I do, maybe. But I don't think that's going to happen."

A horn sounded as the taxi arrived, but he didn't look away from Sara. She had her rules. Rules he couldn't begin to follow. "The taxi's here," he murmured.

She glanced past him. "Yes," she said, and awkwardly took the backpack by its strap. He opened the door for her, then went past her to the cab, put the car seat on the back bench seat, then turned to Sara. "You'll have to belt it in. I've never done it."

She hesitated, then said, "I hate to ask

you this, but could you hold her for just a minute? I'd rather not set her down with the traffic and all."

It was the right thing to do, to help her, but it didn't stop his incredible awkwardness, taking the little girl from her mother and trying to hold her when all she wanted was to go back to her mother. "Mommy! Mommy!" she screamed, her face scrunched up with impending tears while she planted one of her tiny hands right in the middle of E.J.'s chest, pushing with a strength that amazed him.

"Hey, hold on there," he said, trying to make sure he didn't drop her when she almost lurched right out of his grasp. "Oh, come on," he muttered, jiggling her, trying to pat her back, but she was having none of it. Then he looked up and saw the security man watching him with a degree of humor in his expression.

"She's a handful, isn't she…sir?"

He had no idea why the guy thought this was funny. With Sara half in the cab fixing the seat, and the child making passing pedestrians take a second look at the lot of them, he wasn't amused. Then Sara straightened up and turned, reaching for the screaming child. Hayley all but fell into Sara's arms, as if she was escaping a fate worse than death.

"Oh, baby, hush. I was just fixing your car seat," she said, then she looked at E.J. "Edward wasn't going to hurt you."

He exhaled, raking his fingers through his hair. "She's strong," he muttered.

"She's determined," she said, and got into the cab. He watched her strap Hayley in the car seat. Then she turned, reached for the backpack and placed it on her lap. "Thanks again," she said, and went to close the door.

E.J. closed the door for her, then opened the front passenger door and got in. "What are you doing?" Sara asked.

He didn't know, but he wasn't going to stand there and wait for another cab. "I need a cab, too, and it's easier for me to go along in this one," he said without turning.

"Where to, buddy?" the cabbie asked.

"Ask her," E.J. said.

Sara gave her address, then spoke to E.J. "I hope it's not out of your way?"

It was in the diametrically opposite direction from his estate, but he turned and looked at her. "It's right on my way," he lied.

She held his gaze for a moment, then as the cab pulled away from the curb, Hayley grabbed her by the T-shirt and screamed. Sara didn't flinch, just reached over, took her daughter by the hand and eased her hold on the cotton top. Without looking at Hayley, she said, "Be a good girl," and the child sat back in the car seat with a perfect pout on her rosebud lips.

E.J. wasn't going to hold his breath for this child to be a "good girl" anytime soon. And she proved he was prophetic when she threw both hands over her head and brought them down with a dull thud on the padded bar that was in front of her. "Out!" she said. "Out, now!"

"No, honey, you have to stay in there until the car stops," Sara said with admirable restraint, and looked away from E.J. She put her hand over her daughter's on the padded bar, and as E.J. looked out the windshield, he heard her sigh softly.

He shouldn't have gotten into the taxi with her, and he shouldn't be here with her now. She was not part of his world. He needed to be at the estate, calling any number of women he knew in town who wouldn't mind having dinner with him. Women without kids. That should sound good, he thought, but it didn't.

He was aware of Sara speaking softly to her child, but he didn't bother really listening as they drove through the city. It was the tone in her voice, that soft gentleness, that caught his attention. He had no doubt she was a good mother, a caring mother. But that thought hadn't crossed his mind when he'd wanted to see her earlier. Now everything was different. And part of him was disappointed. Strange.

"Just up there," Sara said. "We're in the back house, so pull into the driveway." They were on a narrow street lined with small, old houses, two to a lot, one in front and one behind, with crushed rock where grass should have been, a few trees here and there, and cracked sidewalks. The cab slowed, turned into a narrow driveway, went past a tiny house with peeling yellow paint and stopped behind an old compact car parked in front of a chain-link gate that fronted another small house with oxidized green siding.

E.J. got out and turned to open the back door for Sara. She managed to get Hayley out of the car seat, then slid out and stood with the child on her hip again. "I'll come back for the bag and seat," she said, then went around E.J., past the old car, and pushed the gate back with a squeak of protest from the hinges.

He looked into the cab. "I'll be a few minutes," he told the driver, then grabbed the car seat and backpack and followed Sara. By the time he reached the tiny house, taking the two steps to the front stoop in one long stride, Sara had the door open and was setting Hayley down inside. The child ran off into the house, and Sara turned. He could tell he'd startled her, and especially liked the way her eyes widened and made her look more lovely.

"You didn't have to do that," she murmured, taking her things from him.

He shrugged. "If you had three arms, I wouldn't have."

That brought a slight smile, another thing that he realized only made her more appealing. "Thanks. Now you can make your escape while Hayley is hunting for her doll."

He'd wanted an evening with her, but this wasn't what he'd had in mind. Now it was time he made his escape. He wouldn't look back. But before he said that final goodbye, he was going to do what he'd wanted to since that first glimpse he'd had of her at the café.

He took a step closer, reached out and touched her chin, not missing the way she tensed. But with her hands full, she couldn't do much more than just stare at him. Then he dipped his head and found her lips. Soft, warm lips, parted from surprise, and he knew in that instant that he shouldn't have given in to his impulse. He shouldn't have kissed her. Because he didn't want to stop.

CHAPTER SIX

SARA WAS STUNNED. Stunned that Edward was kissing her, and stunned that she wasn't doing a thing to stop it. She stood there, tasting his lips on hers, while the car seat and backpack fell from her hands with a clatter to the bare wooden floor. Afraid to close her eyes, that this might all be a dream, she watched as he became a blur.

Just then, he pulled back and all she could do was stand there and stare at him. Was she still breathing? He was less than six inches from her, coming into perfect focus, those hazel eyes filled with an intensity that made her tremble.

Suddenly, Hayley screamed "Mommy, Mommy!" from somewhere behind her, and hit Sara in the back of her legs, almost making her knees buckle as she hugged her tiny arms around her.

Sara stared at Edward, saw him grimace slightly, then he moved back, breaking all contact as he distanced himself in every way. "You're leaving," she said flatly, and it wasn't a question.

His hazel eyes flicked over her face once, and for a long, heart-stopping second fixed on her lips, then he said, "Yes," and walked away.

"Mommy!" Hayley screamed, tugging on her jeans, but she didn't move until she heard the taxi door shut behind him and she saw the taxi back out and disappear. Only then did she reach out, close the door with a soft slam, push the car seat to one side with her foot and crouch in front of Hayley. "What's wrong, baby?" she asked.

"Mooney? Mooney gone," Hayley said, her bottom lip unsteady. The old rag doll was the most important toy Hayley had, her first gift from Santa. "All gone," she said dramatically.

"Mooney's in your bed, baby. Look under the sheets," Sara said, then stood as Hayley darted back into her bedroom.

She hadn't kissed anyone except Paul for

a very long time, and the shocking thing was, she couldn't remember ever being shaken like that by a simple kiss. Paul had been good-looking, and he'd been intriguing…at first. He'd known what to say, what to do, and she'd been stupid enough to buy into it. Then Hayley had come along, and by then Sara had known what a mistake her marriage had been.

She pressed her hand to her mouth, then scrubbed it fiercely across her lips. She couldn't remember if they'd talked about children, but she remembered Paul's reaction when she'd gotten pregnant. He hadn't wanted Hayley. He hadn't wanted to be a father. At least Edward was up front about that. And now he was gone. He wasn't coming back. He'd made that clear enough, too. And she didn't want him to. She didn't want to be confused and needy. She wouldn't be.

Hayley streaked out of her room and ran to Sara again, holding the old rag doll. "Mooney," she cried with triumph. "Founded Mooney, Mommy," she said, as

Sara reached down and pulled Hayley into her arms.

"You sure did," Sara breathed, hugging her daughter to her as she closed her eyes. "Good girl. Good girl."

She hugged Hayley for so long that the little girl started to squirm and pushed against her to get free. Then Hayley ran off to find more toys, and Sara stood in the middle of the all-but-bare living room. On still shaky legs, Sara crossed to the television. She snapped it on to cartoons, called out to Hayley that her favorite was on, then went into the kitchen to make dinner.

Edward had come to ask her out to dinner? That made her tremble slightly. All in all, it was a good thing that he'd never asked her. A very good thing, she told herself. And a good thing that Hayley had run into the room when she had. Because for a brief moment, she'd felt a real longing for a nice dinner out, the company of an adult, conversation that was more than single syllables, and something besides macaroni and cheese.

"Then what?" she muttered to herself.

She shook her head sharply, resisted the urge to touch her tongue to her lips just to make very sure the taste of the man was gone, and crossed to take out the package of macaroni and cheese. As she reached for the box she stopped. She hadn't paid him for the taxi. The money was still in her pocket. She groaned.

She didn't want to owe him, but she didn't want to see him again, either. Then she realized she could just put the money in an envelope and leave it for him at the legal department at LynTech. She sighed with relief. She'd do that first thing tomorrow.

AN HOUR LATER, E.J. got back to the estate on the outskirts of the city. He headed into the west wing of the sprawling, multilevel, brick-and-wood structure. The house had more square feet than a stadium and felt about as cavernous at times. The west wing was a house unto itself, with four bedrooms, four baths, full food facilities and a staggered terrace in three levels overlooking rolling pastures and the pool area, as well as the glow of the city in the distance.

E.J. found Martin on the second level of the terrace, working on last-minute details for tomorrow, when all the papers were to be signed, the deal closed. He sidestepped a question about why he was back so early with an offhand, "I was more tired than I thought. I'm going to bed."

Martin put the papers he was reading into his briefcase on the glass-topped patio table. "I think I will in a while."

E.J. nodded. "Good night, then," he said. "Oh, if you want to leave a window open, do it when you go up. Security sets everything at midnight."

"They told me," Martin said.

E.J. headed for his suite at the farthest end of the wing and stepped into the darkened sitting room as he made his way to the bedroom. He pulled open the French door to the balmy night, then changed into swim trunks and padded out onto the higher private terrace and the hot tub positioned for the view. He slipped into the steamy water and sat back, resting his head on the padded edge, and stared up at the sky.

He tried to relax, to just let go, but that lasted about two minutes. He'd always been able to keep business at bay when he wasn't at the offices in Dallas, or in the middle of deals. Business wasn't the center of his life the way it was with most men in his position. But even as he thought that, he wondered what the center of his life was. He didn't have a clue. He knew he was doing this deal with LynTech to unclutter his life, but once it was streamlined, what would he do?

He closed his eyes and thought of Sara. She was tied firmly down with her child and two jobs. He shifted, sinking lower into the steamy water. Sara. He drifted, her image there in his mind, and before he knew or understood where his mind was going, he felt his body tense. The kiss. Touching her. Feeling the silkiness of her skin, a slight trembling in her just before he kissed her. Her eyes. He opened his own quickly and stood up, then got out of the tub. He padded into his bedroom, grabbed a large towel and scrubbed his skin.

Without turning on any lights, he went over to the bed and lay on top of the down-filled duvet. He reached to his right, hitting the remote button on the side table that lifted the large TV out of the cabinet at the foot of the bed and raised it to viewing level. He flipped through channels, then stopped at an old movie he'd seen when he was a kid, a real "shoot 'em up" western, and he stared at the action on the screen.

The last thing he remembered before the dream started was the hero rescuing the fainting maiden from the grips of the bad guy. He pictured himself and Sara. He was leaping off a horse, running toward her, snatching her from the grips of a nebulous villain, faceless and nameless. He rescued her, pulling her back into his arms, feeling her cling to him, her breath mingling with his, her heart beating rapidly against his.

He looked up, and the villain was the man who'd caused trouble at the restaurant, with food all over him. Sara was dressed in her waitress's uniform, her aquamarine eyes wide and brilliant, her smile beautiful. She was touching him, framing his face with her hands, smiling at him, then kissing him with a sweetness that spread warmth through him.

He sank into the dream, relishing the sensation, letting go without any thought to anything but her. A scream ripped through the pleasure, a child's scream. A wordless sound that shattered the moment into a million irretrievable pieces. The child had ruined everything, and E.J. bolted upright, suddenly and jarringly awake in the darkness of the suite.

But the sound was still there, a high, shrill, ear-assaulting siren of a sound. No, it wasn't a child screaming. It was a siren. He scrambled out of bed, grabbing a robe and slipping it on as he hurried through the suite to the hall door. He opened it and Martin was there in pajama bottoms, the siren even louder in the hallway.

"What's going on?" E.J. yelled as he approached the other man, then heard the sound of running feet getting closer.

E.J. turned as two security men came

running toward them. "Sir, are you all right?" the closest one called in a loud voice just as the siren stopped. The silence was almost painful, then the man asked again in a breathless voice, "Are you secure?"

"Yes. What's going on?"

"The alarm was tripped in this wing, and—"

"It's nothing," Martin said. "I accidentally opened the windows in my room. I forgot."

The second security man silently went into Martin's room, then came out and nodded to the other man. The first security guard looked at E.J. "It's secure," he announced.

"Thanks," he said.

"I was looking over the final draft and—" Martin looked at E.J., then past him into E.J.'s suite.

"Well, since I'm awake and you're awake…"

E.J. cut him off. "Forget it. I'm not doing business now."

"Then I'll go back to my room," Martin

said with a slight smile. "You go back to sleep. Sorry for the interruption."

"Yeah," E.J. said, sorry for the interruption, too.

"See you at seven," Martin said as he turned and entered his room with a slight wave over his shoulder.

E.J. returned to the suite and closed the doors behind him. He headed to the built-in bar in the sitting area. He poured himself a glass of water, then went back out onto the terrace and dropped down into one of the canvas chairs by the hot tub. He took a sip of the cool liquid, then cradled the glass in both hands on his stomach.

A dream. Just a dream. But he could still feel the effects of that dream. When he'd left Sara earlier, he was sure that was that. Even though the kiss had rocked him. A kiss was just a kiss. He laughed softly. Sure it was. What a lie. He sat there for a very long time, then went back inside and crawled into bed.

But sleep was a long time coming, with thoughts of Sara still filling his mind. Despite every evasive tactic he knew to stop the thoughts, none worked. He thought about the kid. That should have cut through his delusions and stopped everything, but it didn't.

Even when he slipped into sleep well into the night, Sara was there, but not the way she'd been at first. She slipped in and out of fleeting, elusive dreams, and by the time he woke the next morning, he realized that it didn't matter about the little girl. He wasn't looking to be a stepdad, or even an uncle to the kid. He liked her mother. It was that simple.

Once he was dressed, he exited the suite and knocked on Martin's door. The man opened it almost immediately. "I'm ready. Just let me grab a tie," he said, and hurried back into his room.

As they walked out to the car, E.J. said, "Can you find a really good baby-sitting service for me?"

Martin stopped at the car and turned. "A what?"

"Baby-sitting. Find one that has the best credentials you can, no matter what it costs."

"Can I ask why?" Martin asked as he climbed in the limo.

E.J. slid in after him and closed the door. "LynTech," he told Andrew, his driver, then settled back in the leather. "I want to take a woman out, and I don't want her three-year-old coming along."

"Well, I'll be. You're going to date a woman with a child? A clear breach of your rules, I think."

He shrugged. "They're my rules. I can alter them to suit the occasion. Now I just have to convince the mother to go out with me."

"As if you have to do much convincing to get a woman to go out with you," Martin said.

"She doesn't know who I am," E.J. admitted.

"Who does she think you are?"

"She thinks I work in the legal department at LynTech."

Martin actually laughed, as if E.J. had told him a really good joke. "Sure, of course, you look just like the legal type. Why does she think that?"

"It's a long story. Just find a baby-sitter, okay?"

"No problem," he said. "When do you need one by?"

His business at LynTech would probably take up the whole day. "How about tomorrow evening?"

"Whatever you say," Martin murmured.

Now he just had to convince Sara that dating was okay. That two adults could enjoy each other's company without it having to be complicated. If only he could convince himself.

SARA NEVER GOT A CHANCE to do anything about the money she felt she owed to Edward. But during a rushed day, she thought about the man far too much. The ball plans all but overwhelmed her, and she ended up spending a great deal of time with Marigold Stewart, the party planner, at Marigold's offices in the revitalized downtown area of the city.

But the money was in her pocket the whole time. She'd planned on taking it up to Legal when she went back to pick up

Hayley, but that didn't happen, either. Her meeting with Marigold lasted until so late that Mary ended up bringing Hayley to meet her at Marigold's office around six-thirty.

Mary had been in a hurry, but as she got back in her car to leave, she'd rolled down the window and said, "Oh, by the way, that man, Edward, called down today. He wanted to talk to you."

"What about?" she asked, unable to imagine why he'd want to talk to her. Surely not about the kiss. That was a dead end. Maybe he wanted his money.

"He didn't say, but you might want to call him tomorrow," Mary said, then drove off.

Sara went right home, and as soon as Hayley fell asleep, she crawled into bed. But sleep didn't come. She lay in the darkness, restless and oddly sad. She'd been alone for most of her marriage. Paul had come and gone, spending most of his time with other women. She wondered if there was any man out there who could love Hayley and her unconditionally.

She rolled onto her side, and the tears came silently. She seldom cried. It didn't do any good, and it only drained her. But tears were there as she closed her eyes and hugged her pillow. She hadn't let thoughts like this intrude on her very often. But now they overwhelmed her. She knew why. Edward. The kiss. And she hated him for exposing the things she'd hidden from for what seemed forever.

The next morning, the Lennox Café was busy well past the usual breakfast rush that ended most days around nine-thirty. It wasn't until after ten-thirty that things settled down and Sara was able to breathe. She took a small table that gave her a view of the entry, in case a customer came in, and poured herself a cup of coffee.

She felt the effects of not sleeping well, and that sense of loneliness still lingered. She shouldn't blame the kiss for causing this havoc within her. Maybe it was just having that contact with someone, that sense of connection. Whatever it was, it had lingered into the shadows of night and into the light of the new day.

She took a sip of coffee and knew that as soon as she got to the center, she'd go up to Legal and leave the money for Edward. She'd put the ten dollars in a plain envelope, and she had it in her purse in the locker. She'd get rid of it as soon as she could, then that would end it. Done and over. She took another sip of the steaming coffee and felt a slight shudder run through her. Done.

"Customer," Hughes said as he passed her table. "And no visiting on my time anymore," he added with a dark glance before he kept going to the kitchen.

She looked up, and the hand holding her cup froze on its way to her lips when she saw Edward coming in. Oh, no. She didn't want to see him standing there, wearing jeans and a leather jacket with a collarless white shirt. She didn't want this at all. But she had no choice. She stood, smoothed the apron on her uniform and took a breath to steady herself.

She braced herself, reached for a menu, then crossed to him. She'd do this. She'd smile, speak politely when she got close to him. She'd just say, "Good morning, sir. Bar or restaurant?" and seat him.

He watched her as she approached him, and it made her horribly uncomfortable, but she could deal with that. And she would have, if he hadn't smiled suddenly when she got within a few feet of him. But he did, and she missed her step, stumbled. He reached out, caught her by her upper arm to keep her from falling at his feet.

His grip was light, barely there to steady her, but it could have been a branding iron for the effect it had on her. She regained her balance and jerked back sharply to get free, but the action made the menu slip out of her hand and sent it sailing toward the bar. It hit the surface with a slapping sound, then there was a clatter of glasses hitting one another. She went to retrieve it. "Sorry, Leo," she muttered to the bartender, who was holding it out to her.

She took the menu and went back to Edward, thankful that Hughes hadn't come back out of the kitchen. "Sorry," she muttered tightly. "Bar or restaurant?"

"Where is it safest?" he asked with that smug smile.

She wished she could smile, that she could make light of everything, but she just couldn't. She could barely get the words out. "Bar or restaurant?"

He shrugged. "Restaurant."

She led the way to the first table and motioned for him to sit. "Would you like a drink?" she asked.

"I'd like a different table," he answered.

She looked at him. "What?"

"Not by the door. How about…?" He looked past her. "That table?" he said with a nod toward the space behind her.

She turned and realized he was pointing to the table where the big accident had happened the first time she laid eyes on him. He was teasing her, and she'd had enough. She turned to him and feigned shock. "Oh, sir, that is not a good choice. That's a designated danger area," she said without a smile.

She had the great pleasure of seeing Edward blink, the biggest reaction she'd probably get. The man was so controlled. She stood very still and waited. Then he spoke with an ease that took a bit of the wind out of her sails. "Oh, sure, I forgot. Over there would be much safer," he said, and didn't wait for her to show him to another table. He headed to a table by the tinted windows and sat down.

"Good choice," she muttered, and dropped the menu on the table in front of him. "Now, something to drink?"

"Coffee."

"Good choice," she said again, and headed to get the coffee and the envelope.

When she came back, the envelope was in the pocket of her apron and she had the pot of coffee. She grabbed the key from the tip jar and put it in her pocket, too. Then she crossed and poured his coffee. "Cream and sugar are there," she said, pointing to the silver creamer and sugar set on the table.

"Oh, thanks," he muttered, with more than a tinge of sarcasm.

"Is there a problem?"

"I don't know," he said with narrowed eyes. There was no smile now and it made her feel terrible. She wasn't a sarcastic person who had to one-up anyone. She never had been, but for some reason, he brought that out in her, which didn't make any sense.

"Sorry," she said softly.

"Bad day?"

That took her back. She didn't want sympathy, not from him, not when she had the craziest thought that his sympathy would be wonderful. She stiffened. "Normal," she said.

"You never called me back," he said.

"I didn't know your number."

"I left my cell phone number with the person who answered the phone."

"What did you want?" she asked.

He looked away from her and down at the menu. "What's good?"

He chose to misunderstand and she let it go. "Everything."

His expression softened a bit. "Can you be a bit more specific?"

"The beef au jus is wonderful," she said.

"I'll have that," he said.

She wrote it down, then picked up the

coffeepot and headed to the kitchen. As she stepped through the doors, Hughes was there. "I thought I told you no visiting?"

"Sorry, he didn't know what he wanted."

Hughes eyed her. "Oh, I think he does, but not on my time, understood?"

She cringed at what he was saying, and went to put in the order. She watched Edward on his cell phone through the porthole window. When she finally went back out with his food, he looked up, turned the phone off and put it in his jacket pocket.

"Horseradish?" she asked.

"No, thanks," he said.

She reached into her pocket, took out the key and laid it on the table, along with the overtip to Leo. "You left this the last time you came in and Leo forgot to give you your change."

"Oh, I was looking for that," he said and took the key and money, pushing them into his jacket pocket. "Thank Leo for me."

"Sure," she said, then placed her envelope on the table. "I forgot to pay you for the taxi the other night."

He stared at the envelope, then up at her as he sat back. "No."

"No?"

"No. I don't want your money. It was my treat."

"No, I pay my way," she said, and moved the envelope closer to his plate. She turned and headed back to the kitchen, not stopping until the doors swung shut behind her.

"What's going on with you and that guy?" Hughes asked, startling her. He didn't look happy.

"Nothing. I just got his food for him."

"Keep it that way," he said. "Do your job, Mrs. Flynn. That's what you're paid for." He held up the coffeepot. "And you put this back on the warmer, not on the counter in here. The coffee's tepid and we'll have to make a new pot."

She hadn't even realized she'd done that. "Oh, yes, sir, right away," she said, and took the pot from him, crossing to clean it and make more brew.

She furiously scrubbed the pot, ground the coffee fresh, then measured it into the machine and put in the water. Her hands were less than steady, but she'd gotten the money back to Edward and she hadn't had to hunt him down in Legal. She pushed the button to start the coffee, then went back out.

As she stepped into the restaurant, she stopped in her tracks. The table where Edward had been sitting was empty, the food untouched. She hurried over to it and her heart sank when she saw the envelope where she'd left it, and right beside it were two crisp twenty-dollar bills. An arrow had been drawn on the envelope, pointing to the money, and Edward had scrawled, "For the bill and your tip."

"Oh, no," she breathed. His meal had been fifteen dollars, so that left a twenty-five dollar tip. She looked at the exit, but he was long gone.

She picked up the envelope and the money, pushing it all into her apron pocket, then saw the key. He'd forgotten all about it. Quickly she cleared the untouched food. Now she didn't have a choice. She had the envelope to give him, the key and twenty-five dollars. No, she'd take a twenty-percent tip. She'd earned that, but he'd get the rest back. No matter how long it took to convince him.

CHAPTER SEVEN

AT FOUR O'CLOCK Sara still had the money and key in the pocket of her jeans while she tried to make heads or tails out of the party planner's notes regarding the layout for the ball. She'd understood everything when Marigold had explained it yesterday, but now she was having trouble concentrating.

Sara was in the office, while Mary, Mallory and two other women who worked part-time at the center, were with the children. She heard the laughter and squeals of delight, then music playing loudly. She stared at the plans, forcing herself to focus on them. They were perfectly rendered, but Sara was sure the dimensions in the rooms were wrong.

The ballroom looked large, but if she believed what Marigold had written on the plan, the room cut through two stories of the house and was one hundred feet long and eighty feet wide. That wasn't a ball-room; that was a football stadium. She studied the setup, once again, noting just how much space they had to work with. The tables, the stage, the area where the string ensemble would be seated, including French doors that opened onto a sprawling terrace—it was a lot to take in.

She put the paper down, knowing she'd see it soon enough for herself. Until then, she'd have to take Marigold's word for it. She reached for the guest list, which was growing daily. So far, two hundred of the city's wealthiest had responded and were paying a very large sum for the privilege of spending even more money once they got there. The money they were sure to raise would be staggering. Although, she'd heard more than one person say it would be a "help," just the start for what they needed for both the center and the pediatric wing.

"Sara? How's it going?"

She looked up as Mary came into the of-fice. "I'm just looking at this layout," she said. "These dimensions cannot be right. If they are, this place is unbelievable."

"They're right. Just wait until you stand in that room. It's hard to believe that the owner never uses it. Then again, how many grand balls does a person give?"

"I wouldn't know," she said as she folded the papers.

"You need a break, and now's a good time. The late pickups won't be leaving until five, and it's quiet out there now. Mallory's reading to the children, and some of the other children are putting the finishing touches on their artwork for the ball."

She pressed her hand to her right pocket and felt the folded envelope and the key. "Actually, I need to do something." She came around the desk. "What floor is Legal on?"

"I didn't mean for you to do more work," Mary said quickly as Sara stood. "You need to take a breather."

"Oh, I will take a breather. This isn't business. It's personal. I just don't know what floor Legal's on."

"The nineteenth," someone said from

the door, and Sara looked up to find a tall woman with flaming red hair, dressed in jeans and a snug T-shirt. She smiled at Mary. "I was wondering if Anthony's school van had arrived yet," she said, then glanced at Sara. "I don't think we've met. I'm Brittany Terrell."

"Sara Flynn," she said. "I just started here."

"I'm Anthony's mother, the nine-year-old hoodlum who runs wild around here."

Mary chuckled. "Oh, come now. He's a lovely boy. And no, he hasn't arrived yet."

Brittany smiled. "He is that, yes indeed, very lovely. And speaking of lovely people, have you seen Dad or is he still in that meeting upstairs?"

Mary looked vaguely flustered. "I wouldn't know." She looked at Sara and spoke a bit too quickly. "Mr. Lewis is the man who founded LynTech, and Brittany is his daughter. He's helping out with some company business on the top floor and Brittany is our resident artist. She did the murals on the walls."

"They're wonderful," Sara said.

"I love doing them. And Dad loves being back in the saddle here," Brittany said. "Are you going to Legal?" she asked Mary.

"No, Sara needs to."

She looked at Sara. "It's on the nineteenth floor. I'm heading that way now if you want to join me?"

"Thanks, yes."

Brittany looked at Mary. "When Anthony comes in on the school van, could you tell him I'll be in Matt's office? He can come up and meet me and Dad there."

"Of course," Mary said.

"Ready?" Brittany asked Sara.

"I just have to let my daughter know I'll be gone," she said. "She's out in the main playroom."

"Okay, let's go," Brittany said.

Sara went out to where Hayley was playing with Victoria, the little girl they'd gone to the show with the past Sunday. Victoria was very carefully showing Hayley how to put away the reading books. "Hayley, honey?" Sara said, dropping down by the two little girls. "Mommy has to leave for a few minutes, okay?"

Hayley looked up, but Victoria was the one to speak. "I can watch her," she said in a tiny voice.

Sara smiled at the little girl. "That would be wonderful."

Victoria looked pleased, then turned to Hayley and said, "The blue books go on the blue shelf," and showed Hayley how to do it.

Sara stood, and Brittany said, "She's a doll" as they headed out of the center.

"Thanks," Sara said as they approached the elevators and boarded the nearest one. Brittany hit the button for the nineteenth floor and the twentieth. "You know your way around here," Sara said as the doors closed.

"I was brought up in this place."

"I'm lost once I get above the first floor," Sara admitted with a slight smile. "So I stay downstairs."

"Except to go to Legal?"

That reminded her why she was in the elevator and going up to the nineteenth floor. "Well, I have to drop something off for one of the attorneys."

"Tell me it's not our Mr. Lawrence," she said with a slight grimace. "He's such a windbag and he's been here since the beginning of time. You'll be there until the cows come home listening to him explain why you should have knocked on his door once instead of twice."

Sara laughed. "No, not Lawrence. Edward Jonathan."

There was a soft chime as the elevator stopped and the doors slid open. Brittany shrugged. "I don't think I've ever met him. But they've got so many new people around here. Good luck."

Sara stepped out, the doors slid shut and she was in a reception area that was stylized and sleek, with brushed-stainless-steel-and-glass walls and textured rugs underfoot over polished stone floors. She approached a huge desk directly across from the elevators, and a woman with silver hair and wearing too much makeup looked up at her. "Can I help you?"

"I…" She had her hand in her pocket, clutching the crumpled envelope with the money in it, and remembered that Edward had written on it. "Do you have an envelope?"

The lady reached into a cabinet to her left and handed her an off-white envelope with the LynTech logo in the upper-left corner. "Is one enough?"

"Oh, yes, thanks," she said, and turned her back to the woman while she managed to put the crumpled envelope in it along with the key, then sealed it before she turned back to the woman. "Could I borrow your pen for a moment?"

The woman raised one eyebrow but simply reached for a pen near her elbow and held it out to Sara. Sara scrawled Edward's name on the front, then held the pen and the envelope out to the lady. "Thanks for the pen, and could you make sure Mr. Jonathan gets this envelope?"

The lady took the envelope, glanced at it, then gave it back to Sara. "Sorry, you must have the wrong department. There's no Mr. Jonathan here."

Her phone rang right then and she reached for it. "Legal," she said, then listened.

Sara looked down at the envelope and wondered if she'd heard him wrong about his last name, but she was sure he'd said Jonathan. The woman was explaining something to the person on the phone, frowning as she spoke, then swiveled her chair to turn her back to Sara.

Sara waited for what seemed forever, but the woman never looked back at her. Finally she realized she'd been dismissed, and there was no one else around to ask about Edward. Sara shrugged, then went back to the elevator and hit the down button with a bit more force than she'd intended. The doors opened almost immediately and she was staring directly at the only person in the car. Edward.

For the second time today he popped up where she'd least expected. He reached out and held the door open, then murmured, "Going down?"

She stepped inside, thankful that she didn't trip over the threshold in the process. "Yes," she breathed, and moved to her right until her shoulder pressed to the side wall and she was facing the doors.

"What were you doing up here?" he asked in a low voice, but it strangely seemed to fill the elevator car.

She stared at the doors, determinedly ignoring his reflection just a foot or so from hers in the polished metal. "Looking for you," she said.

"Oh?" was all he said.

She held the envelope out to her left without looking at him. "The taxi money, your change and your key. You forgot all of it when you disappeared at the restaurant."

When he didn't take it, she finally had to look at him. Those hazel eyes were on her, but he didn't make any move to take the envelope. "You're persistent, aren't you?"

"I told you, I pay my way."

"You brought it all the way up here to give it back to me?"

"I was leaving this for you at Legal, but the woman didn't know you, then she took a phone call that lasted forever, and I had to get back to the center before five. But you're here, so you can take it now."

"I don't want it," he said.

She was feeling flustered and pulled her

hand back, pressing the envelope to her middle. "She didn't know you, Edward."

"Who didn't know me?" he asked.

"The gray-haired lady with all the makeup at the reception desk on the nineteenth floor."

"Why should she know me?"

"You said you worked in Legal, and I assumed—"

"Assumption is the straw that broke the camel's back," he pronounced without batting an eyelash.

She stared at him. "That doesn't make any sense."

"No, it doesn't, does it?" He smiled slightly and shook his head. "My dad always sounds so sage, saying stuff like that, but I guess I messed that one up, didn't I?"

"I'd say so." She took a breath and ended up inhaling his essence, that faint scent of leather and maleness, mingling with a subtle aftershave…maybe soap. She didn't know. But she took a much more shallow breath the next time. "But it doesn't change the fact that she didn't know you."

The elevators stopped at the lobby, and

when the doors slid open, a man with thinning red hair and wearing an immaculate navy suit stepped in. "Oh, great, I was looking for you—" he said when he saw Edward.

But Edward cut him off as he grabbed the doors to keep them open. "Martin, I'm leaving. They can take care of the details… under your supervision."

Martin twisted and looked at Sara, as if he hadn't even been aware she was there. "Oh," he said, nodding to her, then turning back to Edward. "Do you need that information now?"

Edward nodded. "If you have it?"

He handed Edward a folded sheet of paper, then said, "I'll see you…when I see you."

"That's the plan," Edward said, then he looked at Sara. "Coming?"

She ducked her head and went past the other man, out into the corridor, still clutching the envelope. Edward touched her arm and she jumped slightly at the contact. "Is there any place we can talk and get this settled?"

She pulled back from his touch, faced him and held out the envelope again. "Just take this and it's settled."

He didn't touch the envelope. Instead, he took her by the arm again and led her down the corridor toward the exit into the parking garage. But before they reached the back door, he turned into a short hallway.

That was when she dug in her heels, forcing him to either stop or drag her. Thankfully, he stopped. She tugged at his hold on her, and he let her go easily. That was when she pressed the envelope into his chest. She felt his heart beating against her hand, and she jerked back. "Just take it," she muttered, clutching the envelope to her middle.

"I told you, I don't want it, but I'll make you a deal."

She shook her head. "No deals, just take it," and she held it out again, being careful not to touch him this time.

He looked down and closed his hand over her hand that held the envelope, and never looked away from her. "A deal," he said, and all she could think of was his touch on her, the way he surrounded her hand so protectively, a mixture of heat and strength. She didn't dare move.

"What kind of deal?" she finally managed to say.

"I'll take the money if you agree to go out to dinner with me tonight."

"No," she said. "I told you before that I don't date."

"What if you had a good baby-sitter?" he asked.

All she had to do was say "I don't like you and I don't want to be with you," and she knew he'd leave. But she couldn't do it. The lies stuck in her throat. "I don't, and I can't go to dinner."

"But what if you had a good baby-sitter?"

"I can't leave Hayley with just anyone, and I don't even know you...not really."

"That's the idea of dinner, talk, get to know each other, isn't it?"

"But I still have Hayley," she said.

She could tell her words finally struck a chord, and he let her go. "You're right, and that would be a problem, if this was about a lifelong commitment. It isn't."

Blunt. "Then there's nothing else to say."

"If I professed that I wanted to take you away from all of this, and marry you and be together until death do us part, you'd go to dinner. But if I'm honest and tell you that I just want to get to know you, you're going to cut me off."

She had no idea why tears were starting to sting her eyes, but she'd made herself a promise. No more mistakes. She'd made such a mistake before, she didn't trust herself not to repeat it. And now there wasn't just her, there was Hayley. She couldn't drag her daughter into something she knew was wrong. He'd been pretty clear about his thoughts on kids, and he obviously thought that they could have a casual date then forget about it and move on. She couldn't. She wouldn't. "I didn't ask you for anything."

"No, I guess you didn't," he said with narrowed eyes.

"Now I have to get back to work." She didn't know when everything had gone from simply repaying him to a horrible skirmish that made her feel shaky and a bit sick to her stomach.

She reached out, pushed the envelope inside his partially zipped jacket, muttered, "Your key's in there, too," then turned and hurried away from him, back out into the main hallway and toward the brightly colored doors of the center.

E.J. WAS NEVER AT A LOSS with women. But Sara was unique. At first, he hadn't wanted her to know who he was because he was hoping to get to know her. He liked her. He liked sparring with her, and looking at her. It had been fun, intriguing, but now he was at a loss. She'd turned him down flat. She'd walked away. No, she'd almost run away.

He went after her, saw her at the doors of the center, then she disappeared inside. E.J. had never been the type who ran after a woman, any woman, but it took all of his control to stay where he was and not go after Sara Flynn.

He groaned, and reached inside his jacket to pull out the envelope. He opened it, took out the key and shoved it in his pocket. What could he have said to her? He didn't want anything complicated. He didn't want a kid pulled into his life, and he wasn't ready to make any sort of commitment to anything more than dinner. He'd been honest. Then she'd dropped him like a bad habit.

He pushed the envelope back in his pocket and went toward the front doors, in desperate need of a lungful of fresh air. He had to calm down and get a grip on himself, then forget about Sara Flynn. But before he realized what he'd done, he reached the primary-colored doors of the center. One of them opened and Mary stepped out.

She saw him and smiled. "Hello. More insurance problems?"

"Oh, no," he said.

"Thank goodness. Everything is so involved as it is. Having the kids take part in the fund-raiser is so complicated, I can't imagine how we'd manage if we had the whole thing to oversee."

Children were going to be running

wildly through his house? "I thought it was an adult gathering?"

"Oh, it is, but we're having the children there at first, for the ceremony part, then we're trying to find another room where the kids can play and have pizza. It's a treat for them. I'm on my way to make sure the company who's donating the pizza knows how much we'll need and I must hurry. Sara's there alone with the kids who get a late pickup." She cocked her head to one side. "Say, can I ask you a favor?"

"What is it?"

"I left a contract on my desk in there. It's not important, but I'd like to have someone with a legal brain look at it before I sign it. Could you possibly go and take a look?"

"Mary, I'm not into contracts," he said.

"Me, neither, but you have a law background and maybe you could see if I'm signing away my life or if it really is a good deal."

She wasn't going to give up. "Okay, I'll take a look."

"Oh, thank you so much. It's in the blue folder on my desk with Heller written on the cover. He's in contracts." She patted him on the arm. "Thank you so much, and help yourself to the coffee. There're cookies somewhere around in there, too. Just ask Sara where they are," she said, and hurried off.

He stared at the doors, then went in, and stopped. He heard a burst of collective laughter, then music and sounds that seemed to be coming from a movie of some sort in the play area. He glanced in that direction as he strode past on his way to the open office door. He stepped in, saw the blue folder and had just reached for it when Sara suddenly appeared out of nowhere.

"What are you doing in here?" she asked, and he turned without picking up the folder.

"I didn't hear you come in," he said.

She made a vague motion behind her at the noise coming from the main room. "That's really loud." She took a step into the room. He knew he shouldn't have come in here. It didn't seem to matter what she said or what she did, just looking at her made his breath tighten in his chest. He felt like some hormone-driven teenager. And he was just as foolish.

"It sure is."

She hesitated, then tipped her head to one side. "I hope you aren't here to give me back that money, because if you are, I'm going to have to—"

He held up a hand. "No, that's a done deal."

She exhaled in a rush. "And we aren't going out to dinner, either, right?"

"No dinner. I didn't come in here to force you into anything." He shrugged. "I guess I should apologize for pushing you like that."

She studied him for a long moment, then shook her head. "Blackmail doesn't sit well with me."

"I didn't mean it that way."

"I just wanted you to take the money I owed you."

"You didn't owe me any—"

"I did," she said, cutting him off. "And please, you said it's a done deal. Can we just forget it?"

"Okay," he said. "I won't bring it up again." Then he found himself saying, "Can we start over?"

Sara wanted nothing more than for this tension to end. She hated that feeling of being on the edge of something, but not really understanding what would happen if she stepped off the precipice. But starting all over seemed fruitless. How could she "start over" something she'd never really begun in the first place?

"Listen, thanks for taking the money and for your help with that man in the restaurant, and thank you for the taxi ride. And thank you for being so honest with me. And I'll be honest with you. There's nothing to start over. There just isn't anything there."

She saw his expression tighten and she braced herself for another argument, but it didn't happen. "If you say so," he murmured tightly, but didn't make a move to leave.

He just watched her for a long moment, then turned and picked up something off the desk. When he turned back to her, he was holding a blue folder. "Hey, that's Mary's," she said.

"Mary asked me to look at this," he said.

"Oh," she said, and felt the heat in her face. "I didn't know."

He came around the desk and stood in front of her. "What did you think I was going to do, leave that envelope for you again?"

Her face burned now. "I'm sorry," she breathed.

He narrowed his gaze, then without warning, reached out and cupped her chin. He ignored her jerk at the contact, and his fingers pressed on her skin. His voice was low and his words cut at her. "What happened to you to make you like this?"

She drew back, breaking the contact, trying to absorb the pain that came with his words. "Who do you think you are?" she whispered.

He leaned toward her, coming so close that she felt his breath brush her face when he spoke. "Someone who can't understand where all this anger is coming from, or why you've decided to cut your life off for your daughter." He paused, then said softly, "But then again, I don't know you, do I? I don't understand."

"No, you don't," she said, hating the way her voice was shaking.

She expected him to turn and walk away, to leave and let her figure out what she was doing. But he didn't. Instead, he looked right at her and said in a low, tense voice, "But I want to understand."

CHAPTER EIGHT

"SARA?"

It was then Sara realized the loud sounds in the other room had stopped and Mary was calling for her. She turned away from Edward and went out the door into the hallway. "I'm here," she called, and saw Mary coming toward her.

"You'll never guess what happened. The pizza company that's donating the food said they'll provide as much as we need, no limit. Isn't that wonderful?" she said.

"That's great," Sara said, then realized that Edward was right behind her.

"Oh, there you are," Mary said to Edward. "Did you get a chance to look at the paperwork?"

"Can I take it with me?" he asked.

"Absolutely. I don't need to make a decision until tomorrow or the next day."

Edward was right beside her now, and Sara felt him brush her arm. Then she caught a peripheral glimpse of the blue folder in his hands. "I'll get it back to you tomorrow, then?" he said.

"That would be great. I'm just no good when it comes to legal stuff."

"I'll get back to the children," Sara said, and she hurried into the main room. Thankfully Edward left moments later, striding past without glancing at where she sat by the tree. She exhaled a breath she hadn't realized she'd been holding, then went to get Hayley and head home.

Edward didn't show up at the restaurant the next day, or at the center, and Sara was just beginning to relax a bit. She was helping Hayley and Victoria pick up toys after the other kids had all left, and glanced at the clock. It was almost six. Soon she could leave.

Mary called out to her. "Sara?"

She turned and felt her chest tighten. Edward was standing there. She hadn't seen him come in this time, either. He wore his leather jacket over a gray collarless shirt, along with jeans and boots. He looked the same as always, but her reaction seemed to get more intense every time she saw him. She hesitated crossing to where the two of them stood, but short of ignoring Mary, she didn't have a choice.

"I was just putting away the last of the toys," she said to Mary. "And everyone's been picked up but Victoria."

"She's staying with me for a while," Mary said. "And I needed to ask you for a favor tonight."

She wanted to tell Mary that all she wanted to do was go home and crawl into bed. Instead she said, "What do you need?"

"Hayley. I offered to watch Victoria for Rain and Jack, good friends of mine. Big things are going on with them," she said with a smile. "They need time to make plans for their new life, and Victoria would love to have Hayley come join us, if it's okay with you. We're going to do some serious artwork here and order food. I'll bring Hayley to your place…." She glanced at her watch. "How about by eight?"

Sara had met Rain—a psychologist who

looked a bit like a hippie—when she'd come to pick up Victoria one day. And Hayley loved Victoria. The idea of being alone was, on the one hand, unsettling, but on the other, very appealing. She'd have some long overdue time alone. "Are you sure you're up to that?" she asked.

"Absolutely. And those two kids are terrific together. You'd be doing me a favor if you let Hayley stay."

"I think Hayley would love it," Sara said, feeling a bit ashamed at her relief to have time to herself.

"Wonderful. I'll just go and tell Hayley and Victoria about our plans, and you can get going. I'll see you at eight." Mary headed toward the two girls, who were carefully furnishing a big wooden dollhouse.

Sara turned and almost bumped into Edward. "Sorry," she muttered, and went around him, over to the toy bins. She dumped the toys in the closest container, then turned and found herself facing Edward. "Did you read the contract for Mary?"

"Sure did," he said. "It looks fine to me."

"I'll bet she's relieved," she said, crossing to drop more toys in the bins.

Hayley chose that moment to run at Sara. "Mommy, Mommy!" she yelled, reaching to tug on her shirt.

Sara crouched by her daughter. "I see Mary told you about your big night?"

Hayley nodded vigorously. "Getting pizza!" she announced with the same enthusiasm someone would have if they'd won a million dollars.

"That's terrific. Mary will bring you home later. Have a wonderful time."

"Huh!" she said with another nod, then she streaked back to where Mary was talking to Victoria.

She straightened, and it seemed as if Edward was even closer than he'd been before. "I need to get going," she said quickly, and turned, heading toward the office to get her purse.

She felt him follow her.

"Sara?" Edward said as she went into the office.

She grabbed the backpack, made sure her purse was in it and grabbed her keys, then turned, intent on going past Edward and getting out of there. But he didn't let that happen. He stood in the door, effectively blocking her from leaving. "Could you move, please?" she asked, staring at his chest.

"No."

She closed her eyes so tightly that colors exploded behind her lids, and she held her backpack in a death grip. "Let me go."

He didn't say anything. She opened her eyes and found herself watching his shirt move slightly with each steady breath he took. "I'll let you go," he said.

That brought her gaze up to his, and she wished she knew why he frightened her so much. No, not him, but the way he could make her feel. The thoughts he could make her think by just being there. "Thanks," she said, and made an attempt to go around him. He startled her by moving back, letting her pass, and she strode down the hallway to the back entrance.

She didn't stop until she was in the parking garage and the door closed behind her. Mary had given her a sticker for her car so she could park back here, and she was thankful for it now. She went right to her old car, got in and started it. Then she allowed herself to sink into the seat and take several deep breaths. She closed her eyes, thankful that her heart was slowing and breathing was easier.

She had some time alone and wanted to make the most of it. Pushing the idling car in gear she drove out of the parking garage and into the early evening streets of Houston.

Driving slowly due to the heavy traffic, Sara turned on the radio. But when she looked up again, the car in front of her had stopped dead. She hit her brakes, skidding slightly, stopping mere inches from the other car. Before she could breathe a sigh of relief, a banging lurch sent her forward and back, thanks to her seat belt. Someone had hit her from behind.

"Are you all right?" An elderly man, pale as a ghost, was standing at her window, knocking.

She lowered the glass and said, "I...I

guess so," then undid her seat belt and reached to open the door.

The man stood back and started apologizing. "I am so sorry, dear, so very sorry. I...I didn't see you stop and I..." He threw his hands out in a futile gesture. "I'm sorry."

She turned and saw an all-black luxury sedan, its front bumper lifted at a strange angle off the ground. Sara hurried to take a closer look and felt her heart sink when she saw the whole back of her car was caved in, the bumper half off, lying partly on the pavement, the taillights smashed and the trunk lid looking for all the world as if some giant hand had folded it in and up.

"Oh, no," she breathed. The old car was what she depended on. It had brought her and Hayley all the way from Chicago to Houston, and it had never let her down, despite its age. She didn't know what she was going to do.

"Miss, please don't cry," the elderly man was saying over the beeping of impatient horns. "It will be okay."

She brushed at her eyes. "I'm not sure...."

She wished she knew what she should do, that someone else would take care of it, but that wasn't going to happen. She'd been the one to fix things for as long as she could remember. But then, out of nowhere, her wish came true.

Edward was walking toward her and she felt a tremendous sense of relief that almost made her giddy.

"Sara, what's going on?"

The old man turned to Edward, dwarfed by the younger man. "Sir, I'm truly sorry. It was an accident." He motioned to the two cars, and Edward glanced at the destruction. He moved closer to Sara but didn't touch her. If he had, she probably would have collapsed in his arms.

"Are you okay?" he asked in a low voice.

She managed to nod. "I'm okay, but… but my car isn't."

He turned to the elderly man. "What happened?"

"She just stopped and I didn't see her until it was too late," he said, clasping and unclasping his hands.

"Well, we need to call the police," Edward said.

"Oh, no, that's not necessary. I'll take care of everything," the old man said earnestly.

"Then let's get everything over to the side of the road," Edward said, and moved to her car. He opened the door, reached in, then started to push it single-handedly toward the curb. Luckily it rolled easily, and it nosed into the curb without too much trouble. The old man drove his own.

Sara noticed that the idling luxury car was barely scratched, with just a small dent on its front bumper. But her car looked contorted and as though it would fall apart any minute. "I know this is my fault, and I'll make it right," the old man said.

Edward looked at Sara. "Do you have your insurance card?"

Her purse was in the car. "I'll...I'll get it," she stammered, and managed to open the car door to find her wallet but couldn't seem to get the card out of the plastic sleeve. Edward reached around her, took her wallet from her hands and got the card out. He glanced at it, then looked up at her.

"This is expired."

Her heart lurched painfully. "Oh, no," she whispered. "I forgot to renew it."

He reached out, barely brushing her chin with the tips of his fingers, and all that did was increase her trembling. "Relax, it's not the end of the world," he said.

She leaned her elbows on the roof of her car and buried her face in her hands. Taking several breaths, she tried to calm down. This wasn't fatal. It just felt that way. She had no way to get around if her car was out of commission, and she feared that as old and as banged up as the car was before the accident, any insurance company would write it off as a total loss and offer her a few hundred dollars, even if it was the old man's fault.

She heard Edward talking to the old man, then his hand touched her back. "Sara, let's go." It was a strong hand. A gentle hand. And a hand that she needed very much at that moment. She looked at Edward. "What about my car?"

He handed her a folded piece of paper. "Here's all of his information. I called a tow for your car. They'll take it to the repair shop for an estimate."

That all sounded nice, but it only made her stomach sink. "So, the car…do you think it's pretty much totaled?"

Edward smiled faintly. "Pretty much."

"Oh," she breathed, and the shaking grew worse.

"Hey, it's okay," Edward said, and as if it was the most natural thing in the world, he slipped his arm around her and pulled her to his side. "It's okay," he repeated.

"No, it's not," she said in a flat voice. "Nothing's right." She watched Mr. Row, according to the information Edward had handed her, pull away from the curb slowly.

Edward took her toward a car that looked like a limousine, black and sleek and longer than normal. A man opened the door for them and they crawled inside.

Sara fell onto a soft leather seat and turned to Edward. "I can't just leave my things like that," she said.

"What do you need from the car?" he asked.

"My backpack and my wallet and my laundry."

He headed to her car and in less than a minute, he placed the laundry basket on the seat and handed her the backpack. "I put the wallet in there. Don't worry. The tow company said they'll take care of everything. You can go by tomorrow and get anything else you need." He closed the door. "Right now what you need is to relax and get your bearings."

She sank back and stared at the ceiling of the luxury car. "My bearings? That's a joke," she muttered.

Edward spoke to the driver, saying something about a "nice, quiet restaurant," and Sara bolted upright. "Oh, no," she said.

Edward touched her hand and said evenly, "You need to eat as well as relax."

She knew that being in this car with Edward was fogging her mind and her reason. Prolonging this wasn't a good idea. "No, I just need to go home. Straight home. No restaurants."

He startled her by chuckling softly. "Take the lady home, Andrew," he said.

"What's so funny?" she asked.

"You. You never stop making up rules, do you. I bet that drove your ex-husband nuts."

Now she felt sick. "Someone had to make up rules."

"So you did?"

"I just expected Paul to abide by simple rules, like telling the truth. Or spending time with his child and coming home at night instead of being gone for weeks on end. Things that most people take for granted." She exhaled on a shudder. "He didn't think rules were meant for him, but I didn't realize that until it was too late. I ended up with *two* kids on my hands, Hayley, and Paul, who didn't want to be tied to anything...or anyone."

"So, he left?" he asked.

"He didn't want to be with someone who put demands on him in any way. And he always found any number of women willing to ignore the rules...before and after our divorce."

Sara waited for the pain that always came with that admission, but for once it wasn't cutting and horrible, just a simple, dull ache. More a regret than a real pain.

E.J. heard what she said but found it hard to believe that any man would look at other women when he had Sara. "He sounds like a jerk," he said with real understatement.

"See, you figured that out in a matter of minutes," she said. "It took me a lot longer."

"He's gone? He doesn't help you at all?"

"No, he doesn't help," she said flatly, her usual spark disappearing as she spoke about her ex-husband. "He came and went, whenever the spirit moved him, or whenever he needed money or a place to regroup. I finally filed for divorce, and he came back, signed the papers, took what he needed, then left again. The one thing I really hated was, he never said goodbye to Hayley, never. He just left." He saw the way her fingers were pushing into the canvas of her backpack.

"Where is he?"

"When we left Chicago, he was heading for Los Angeles for an audition with some band. His last words were, he didn't have anything holding him back now, no burdens that could ruin his chance to make it big."

He considered her a "burden"? That thought brought an instant anger that ate at his middle, anger at a man he'd never met and never wanted to meet. "It sounds as if you're better off without him."

"We are, but that wasn't the plan. I thought we'd be a family, have a home and…" She shrugged. "That wasn't what he wanted."

He felt the sadness weighing heavily at her admission. "But that was what you wanted, wasn't it?"

Her hands stilled. "Yes, but I learned my lesson."

"Which is?"

She shrugged, a faint, vulnerable action. "To get past the dreams and face facts."

"So, dreams just go by the wayside?" he asked.

She looked up at him, and he could see

the pain in her eyes. "For now, or maybe they get replaced with other dreams."

"Such as?"

"A good life for Hayley, to make sure she's okay and happy."

He wanted to say something offhand, such as "How noble," but he couldn't make fun of her sincerity. He didn't understand it, but he couldn't demean it, either. "And what about you?"

"What about me? I got us into this mess in our lives, so it's up to me to fix it."

"How do you do that?"

She exhaled on a sigh. "I'm figuring that out as I go along," she said in a low voice. "I'm figuring out what to do, how to do it. I'm putting my priorities in order, and I'm not going to trust someone just because they say the right thing, or smile at the right time."

He finally understood why she'd refused dinner with him, why she'd pushed him back and wouldn't give an inch. On the surface it was about the child, but at the bottom of it all was trust. She'd trusted the jerk she'd married and been hurt. Now she didn't trust anyone, including herself. "That sounds tough," he said.

"I know you don't understand this, but when you have a child, it just plain changes everything."

"I'll just have to take your word for it." He hesitated but had to know more. "Why did you marry that guy?"

She didn't say anything at first, then answered him in a low voice while she stared at her hands on the backpack. "Of course I thought I loved him. I don't have any family. I was by myself, and Paul walked into my life, and he was nice, and he smiled at the right times, and we had fun. He seemed smart, as if he knew where he was going. Then he asked me to marry him."

"Why did he ask if he didn't want to be married?"

"I never figured that one out. Maybe he thought it would be one long party? That we'd have a good time and never stop? Maybe he thought he'd found someone to take care of him? I don't know. I never asked him."

"Do you still love him?"

Her expression tightened even more and she shook her head. "No. I don't think I ever did, now. Maybe it's all a lie."

"What is?"

"You know, that 'can't eat, can't sleep, can't live without you' fantasy that people say is there if you really love someone."

"Obviously, you're living without him," he said.

She blinked, and he realized that her eyes were a bit too bright. Tears? He could see that her hands weren't really steady, and she had to swallow hard before continuing. "Of course I am. People don't die from broken hearts."

"That's a relief," he said, trying to make a joke and break the tension.

"You've never been in love, have you?" she asked, stunning him even though the question was said in a low, slightly unsteady voice.

He shrugged. "I've had…relationships," he said, and couldn't believe the defensiveness he heard in his own voice.

"But never married?" she asked.

He shook his head. "No, never."

She trembled suddenly, then let go of her backpack to hug her arms around herself.

"What?"

"Hayley, Hayley could have been with me when I had the accident tonight, and…" She trembled convulsively and closed her eyes tightly. "If she'd been with me…"

"She wasn't," he said quickly.

He saw her taking quick, shallow breaths, then tears slipped from her closed eyes. "What if I'd been…if it hadn't been such a minor thing? I'm all she's got. I couldn't…"

She started to shake all over, and he reached for her. At first she sat ramrod straight, shaking so hard that he was getting worried. Then she just collapsed, falling into his chest and letting him hold her.

He patted her back and felt her hair brush across his chin. "Hayley's with Mary, and she's fine," he said. "You're okay. This is shock. It's just the accident finally sinking in."

She had his shirt in her hands now, closed tightly in her fists, and her forehead pressed hard against his chest. "I never…

never...cry...." Her voice broke, and she started to cry, huge, wrenching sobs.

He held her while she cried, stroking her back and trying to figure out what to do, what to say to make it better for her. But all he could do was hold her. When Andrew looked back, motioning that they were almost at her house, E.J. made a circling motion and they kept driving. Finally he felt her exhale on a shuddering sigh, and she gradually stilled, resting against him for a long moment.

She slowly eased back, and he looked down into her pale face. "Are you okay?" he asked, fighting the urge to kiss the dampness on her cheeks.

He realized right then that his motives for holding her hadn't exactly been altruistic. Not even close.

"I'm sorry," she whispered, and let go of her grip on his shirt, then frowned at the crushed cotton and tried to smooth it. "This is a first for me, believe me," she said, and hiccuped softly.

He let himself reach out and brush her cheek, then smoothed back a tendril of hair clinging at her temple. In that moment, he knew that this was a first for him, too. He'd never felt as if he wanted to take away all the hurts in another person's world, or to hold that person and never let go. Until now.

CHAPTER NINE

SARA HATED THAT she'd acted this way in front of this man. Edward was watching her, his eyes narrowed, and she was sure he was horrified by her actions. She'd been terrified for Hayley. If anything happened to her, Hayley would have no one. Paul couldn't be depended on to do anything, and that left her with the sole responsibility. It chilled her to even think of Paul being responsible for Hayley.

Edward moved back, putting distance between them, and she did the same. She couldn't cling to anyone, let alone this man. "Shock?" she asked, recalling his earlier words. "Do you think so?"

"I'm no expert, but that would be my guess."

Okay, she could live with that as an explanation of why she'd broken down and cried, and had held on to Edward for dear life. She'd accept it, but she didn't believe it. Not really. There was more going on than she could begin to comprehend, both because of Hayley and because of this man. She looked away from Edward and saw her backpack had slid onto the floor. She reached for it, pulling it back on her lap. "I guess I have too much of an imagination, too," she said with a sigh as she sat back. "I had horrible images…." She bit her lip as the horror returned, making her chest tighten. "I'm all Hayley has," she managed to say.

"Don't you have any family here or back where you came from?"

"An aunt somewhere in New York, and some cousins that I've never met. I never knew my father. He was gone long before I can remember anything, and my mother…" She shrugged. "She's not a factor in any of this."

"She's dead?"

"Oh, no, she's alive. But she's…" She didn't have a clue why she was telling him anything about her mother. "She's got this new life with a new husband, and he's younger than her, and having a daughter who's twenty-eight didn't sit well with her. Then having a grandchild, well, that about did her in." She almost laughed remembering her mother's horror when she found out she'd become a grandmother. "She can't deal with it. I think she'd do the right thing by Hayley if I was gone, but I don't want her bringing Hayley up."

"And your ex wouldn't volunteer, would he?"

Now she did laugh, but it sounded so brittle. "Paul? No, he's not in the picture."

"So, your plan is to either go it alone, or get married to someone who'll be a father for Hayley?"

"Yes."

The car slowed and the driver glanced back at Edward. "Sir? We're getting close to the lady's house."

"Good," he said, the word tinged with what Sara thought sounded like relief.

She looked out the side window, knowing the limousine looked very out of place in her neighborhood. "Do they provide a limo for everyone who works at LynTech?"

"No, of course not, but my car's...not available at the moment, so I get to use this when I need it."

"And Andrew comes with it?"

"That's his job," he said.

Sara directed Andrew and he pulled into her drive. Edward got out, and Sara followed, expecting him to say good-night and get right back in the limo. But he didn't. Instead, after speaking with the driver, he followed her through the gate and to the stoop. There was complete silence once she had opened the door.

"Thanks for everything," she said. But as she turned to face him, her legs buckled and she started to slide to the floor.

Edward caught her by either arm. "Hey, take it easy," he whispered as he steadied her against him.

"Oh, no," she whispered, her legs feeling like jelly. She couldn't have stood on her own if her life had depended on it.

Before she realized what he was doing, Edward was lifting her into his arms and carrying her into the house. "Where's your bedroom?" Before she could protest, he said, "Ah, found it."

Edward carried her to the mattress that sat on the floor and eased her down onto the unmade sheets, getting to his knees in the process.

Being with him was so wrong, but she felt too weak to do anything but sink back in the pillow. His features were softened by the shadows in the room, and thankfully he moved back, but he didn't get off of the mattress. "You need to eat, or at least drink something."

She knew there wasn't much in the refrigerator beyond bread, peanut butter, leftover macaroni and cheese and milk. "Water, please," she said, and when Edward got up to go into the kitchen, she pushed herself into a sitting position with her back against the cold wall.

He returned quickly with a glass of water. She took it, sipped the coolness, then put it on the floor by the lamp. "Thanks. I'm okay now. I just got light-headed or something."

Once again, she expected him to leave, but he didn't. Instead, he sat on the edge of the mattress and looked around the room. "Not one for furniture, are you?" he asked as he looked back at her.

"There wasn't much room in my car, so furniture wasn't an option. You saw how small it is."

"You came all the way from Chicago in that thing?"

"Without a problem," she said. "That's why I need that car back. It's really important."

E.J. watched Sara, listening to her and knowing that he should gracefully bow out now. But he was worried about leaving her alone until he was sure she wasn't going to faint. Her car was a goner, he knew that. And no insurance company would agree to fix it. "It might be a good excuse to get a new one," he offered.

That brought a shadowy smile, but it was more wry than humorous. "Sure, and pigs fly. Do you know what a new car costs these days, even a used one?"

He knew what they cost ten years ago,

but since then he hadn't paid any attention to such things. "There's financing."

"You have to have credit for that," she said.

"How long did you say you've been in Houston?" he asked, to divert her attention and maybe to divert his own. She kept moving her head from side to side, as if her neck was stiff and she was testing it.

"Two months," she said, rotating her head slowly down, then up.

"You left everything in Chicago?"

"Just about," she said.

"He got it all?"

"Oh, no, I sold the rest to get the money to come out here."

"Why Houston?"

"I had a friend here. In fact, this was her place. But I'd barely arrived before she got transferred to the West Coast and had to pack up and leave. So her furniture went with her." She shrugged. "I took over the lease and got a few things for us."

"You don't know anyone else here?"

"Mary and the people at the center, and

a few people at the café." She hesitated. "And you."

"Then why did you come here?"

She shrugged, and he could see her stop in mid action, then release a breath. "Why not? I wanted to get out of Chicago and I knew Cindy from high school, and it's warm here most of the time." She exhaled again. "How about you? Do you have family here?"

"Just my dad," he said at the same time his cell phone rang. He checked the number on the lit LED screen and answered. "Speak of the devil," he muttered to Sara, then spoke into the phone. "What's going on, Dad?"

"Well, Sonny, I hadn't heard from you for a few days and I know the deal's a hard one. I expected you'd give me a rundown on it."

He'd never given him a "rundown" on any deal, either in the process of being made, or once it was finished. "It's going fine. Was there anything else you wanted to know?"

There was a pause. "Well, I was talking

to Martin and he says that you're playing
some kind of game with a pretty young
thing down there."

"Oh, Ray, he's got no right to—"

"He sure enough did. You're my son,
and it's my business if you're sidling up
to some woman who could be the mother
of my future grandkids."

E.J. looked at Sara, grateful she couldn't
read his mind. "Dad, you're out of line,"
he said, getting up and moving over to the
door.

"It's in my interests to know how long
I'm going to have to hang on for you to get
the idea and do the right thing."

"Right now, I'm hanging up on you,"
he said, but waited without hitting the end
button.

"Hey, Sonny, sorry," Ray said quickly.
"I'm here all alone and I was thinking that
I might like a little trip south."

That's all he needed, to have Ray hanging out at the estate and asking even more
questions. "Stay put for now."

"I was thinking that the party at the

place might be a good thing to go to. You know, to make a contribution to the kids?"

"We'll talk this over later."

"Whatever you say, Sonny," Ray said far too easily, and hung up.

Sara was watching him and had obviously been listening in on his conversation. He started to push his phone back into his jacket pocket, but it rang again. He expected Ray, but it was the limo driver. "Yes?"

"Sir, I just got a call from Mr. Griggs. He's at a downtown office and needs a ride."

"Go and get him."

"Should I come back for you?"

"Yes. Just call when you get back." He put his phone away and sat back down on the mattress edge, a few feet from where Sara sat. "Sorry about that," he said, then asked, "Are you okay? Your neck bothering you or anything?"

"It's tight," she said, touching her shoulder with her fingers. "Maybe the muscles are a bit sore."

"Turn around with your back to me," he said, moving closer to her.

"Why?" she asked.

"Trust me," he murmured.

She was very still, then shifted and turned, and he was behind her. He got on his knees, then touched her. He closed his eyes, working his fingers into the tight muscles of her shoulders and neck. "Your muscles are in knots," he said, massaging from her shoulder to her neck.

"Is that helping?" he asked.

She sighed. "It's wonderful."

He felt the heat of her body through her top and the delicate bones of her shoulders under his fingers. And something meant to be therapeutic became something more. She sighed with what he could only guess was pleasure and he felt his body begin to tense. "Better?" he asked.

"Mmm."

He opened his eyes as her head lolled forward, and her neck was exposed, the gentle sweeping line, the smooth skin. "I'll take that as yes?" he murmured.

She shifted, turning around to face him. "Yes," she whispered. "Better. Thanks."

He sat back on his heels. The shadows softened her expression and fell in the hollow of her throat. He touched her cheek with just the tip of his forefinger, but the contact was startlingly intense. He stilled, not breathing, then her hand lifted and covered his. "It's better," she whispered, but he knew that was a lie. This wasn't better. In fact, somewhere along the way, he'd fallen into an area that was downright hazardous.

Then her lips parted, and he ignored the hazards. He ignored everything except her, and her lips. He leaned toward her, then found her lips with his, the softness and heat. If he'd ever thought he'd be in control with her, he'd been dead wrong. The instant he felt her response, nothing mattered. His hand lowered to her back, pulling her closer and they clung to each other, on their knees, on the mattress, their bodies molding together.

Sara had known all along that if Edward kissed her again, her control would be gone, and her need to be touched and held would overwhelm her. And she'd been right, terrifyingly right. The moment she felt his lips and his hands on her, she found herself melting toward him. Being so close to him made her want the impossible—a life where a touch was important, where being with someone drove away the loneliness.

Her life had been empty, except for Hayley, for so long. But now, for these fleeting moments, it wasn't empty at all. It was full, and the loneliness she'd endured for what seemed forever was melting away. Edward held her close, his hands running down her back.

Then a horn sounded. A door slammed. The doorbell rang. Mary and Hayley. "Oh, no," she breathed, pushing back hard, twisting away from Edward and scrambling awkwardly to her feet. Her unsteady hands straightened her hair, and she didn't dare look back as she hurried out of the bedroom. She couldn't. She was horrified that she'd let herself get so caught up in that kiss. Horrified that the man could

touch her on such a basic level and horrified that she wasn't any different at all.

She hadn't learned. She still went with
her feelings. She jumped in feetfirst, and
she couldn't. It terrified her to think of how
close she'd come to destroying her carefully built new world.

"Sara?" she heard Edward say as she
snapped on the living room light. Then he
was there, right behind her, and she shook
her head. "Sara, just a minute."

"No," she muttered, her teeth clenched
and her heart aching. "No." She crossed to
the door, thankful her legs supported her
this time. There was another knock.

"Sara?" Mary called out and knocked
again. "Are you in there?"

She hesitated, then made herself look
at Edward. Thankfully he was far enough
away from her that she could almost think
rationally. "It's Hayley," she said, hating
the tightness in her voice.

He didn't say anything. He just stood
there, then when Mary knocked again, he
glanced at the door. Sara took a breath,
then called out, "I'm here!"

But she couldn't make herself open the door. She couldn't move. She was so sure if she opened the door, Mary would take one look at them and think the worst. And she couldn't bear that.

"Let us in," Mary called, then Hayley chimed in, "Mommy!"

Before she realized what he was doing, Edward went past her and opened the door. He seemed so sane, so normal, smiling at Mary, saying hello, and explaining why her car wasn't out there, and how he'd brought her home. He was saying Sara would explain it to her. Meanwhile, Hayley grabbed her around the legs, babbling about the painting and Victoria and pizza and a nice man who had driven them over here.

She tried to sort out the words, to get a handle on what was going on, then Mary's face was filled with concern. "What trouble?" Mary asked. "What happened?"

Sara hesitated, then shook her head, not about to tell her anything in front of Hayley. "I'll explain later."

But Mary didn't let it go. She turned to Edward. "Can you take Hayley into her room and find a doll that she's been asking for?"

E.J. looked at the little girl, and almost said he was leaving before he got himself tangled up even more with this woman. But he surprised himself by not running. He wasn't done here, and if taking the child into the other room while Sara told Mary about the accident would buy him more time, he'd do it. "Where's this doll?" he asked Hayley.

She wiggled out of her mother's hold and hit the floor running. He went after her. The child's room was the same size as Sara's, but the mattress on the floor was smaller and blankets were bunched at the foot of it, pillows at the top. Toys were scattered on the hardwood floor, and a small doorless closet with shelves held folded clothing and pairs of small shoes.

Hayley ran over to the mattress and tugged at the sheets that were tangled near the bottom of it. "Mooney!" she yelled, then almost buried herself in the linen as she rummaged around.

E.J. crossed to her, crouched by the mat-

tress and saw what looked like the foot
of a rag doll protruding from three pillows banked near the top. He reached for
it, tugged the doll free of the pillows, then
held it up to Hayley. "Is this Mooney?" he
asked.

She turned, and in that moment, she
looked just like Sara. Her blue eyes were
huge, and her mouth formed an O. Odd,
because he'd never been the type to look
at anyone's kids and try to see the parents in them. But without trying, he'd seen
the resemblance and was overwhelmed.
He tossed her the doll and found himself
smiling at the way she scrambled to get to
it and gather it into her arms.

She hugged the doll to her. "Oh,
Mooney," she crooned in a soft voice. "My
Mooney."

He had to admit that she was cute, that
she made him smile. That was more than
just about any kid had ever done to him.
He was attracted to Sara in a way that left
him shaken, his body tense and uneasy.
But that was it. He didn't intend to be any-

thing more to this kid than a doll finder. That he could handle.

He sank down on the mattress. Hayley picked up a stuffed rabbit and held it out to him by one ear, so he took it. She was off to get more toys. Meanwhile, he was aware of the two women talking in the other room, words that he couldn't make out and didn't try to. Then he clearly heard the voice of a man.

"I was beginning to wonder if you got lost," the man said. Robert Lewis. He was here, one room away, and all E.J. had to do was walk out there and Sara would know everything. He wasn't sure why he hadn't told her who he was by now. That was something else that didn't make sense. Even if she knew he was E. J. Sommers, he didn't think it would change her mind about much of anything. The woman was stubborn and focused. He wished he was as focused.

But he didn't go out there. He didn't even know why. He stayed with Hayley, letting her pile toys at his feet while he listened. Mary was telling Robert about the accident, and how sweet Edward had been to help Sara. Then Robert asked, "Is there anything I can do?"

Sara spoke quickly. "Oh, no, thank you."

Hayley threw a sock puppet at E.J., then was off to get some blocks. Robert was asking, "Are you ready to go?" He sounded a bit impatient, which wasn't like Robert.

Mary was speaking now, asking Sara if she needed anything else, and Sara was thanking her for taking Hayley for a while. Then Mary called, "Good night, Edward."

"Good night," he called without moving.

The door opened, and the voices faded away. Sara looked into the room, and he met her gaze. Suddenly she made a dive toward him and before he could register what she was doing, she was between him and Hayley, deftly fielding a wooden block the child had thrown at him.

"Got it," she breathed, then turned to E.J. "Sorry, she's in this throwing phase."

Sara was acting as if nothing had happened, nothing at all, except a near miss to the head with a block. "Obviously you're feeling better," he said, pushing to his feet and letting the toys fall around him.

Sara looked up at him. "Sorry you got stuck watching her."

He almost said "Me, too," but didn't. "She's okay. A bit dangerous, but basically okay."

Sara nibbled on her bottom lip, and E.J. was certain he could still taste her on his own lips. "You're leaving."

It wasn't a question, but a statement. And he stood there. He'd run into cement walls that had more give in them than this woman. "I guess I am," he breathed.

He looked at Hayley, said, "Take care of Mooney," and moved past Sara and out of the bedroom. She was there, behind him. He felt her before he heard her, the way he had that first day at the center, and for a moment he thought she was coming to ask him to stay. But when he turned, that foolish hope was dashed. "Mary said there wasn't a car out there when she got here with Robert. Where's the limo?"

He'd forgotten about Andrew leaving. "I

forgot," he said, and called the driver, who said he'd be by in five minutes.

"He had to leave, but he'll be back. Let's talk."

She shifted from foot to foot, then shook her head. "You can wait outside," she said.

Frustration ripped through him. "Sara, what on earth—"

"Keep your voice down," she hissed.

He went closer to her, then reached out, framing her face with his hands. She jerked at the contact, but finally stood very still under his touch. "Listen to me, and understand something. I can walk out that door now and never come back, and maybe I should. But I don't want to. I want to get to know you, to figure out what's going on with us."

She closed her eyes. "There is no 'us,'" she said tightly.

"Then I don't know what to call the thing that happens every time we're around each other. You give it a name."

Her eyes, those incredible aquamarine eyes, opened wide. "Chemistry?"

"I can't argue with that," he murmured. "But don't you want to know? I sure do."

She trembled. "I can't."

He regrouped, trying to figure this out as he went along. "Okay, what if we do it this way? Hayley stays out of it. I won't do anything to interfere or intrude in her life. Can we do that?"

Her tongue touched her lips, and his body tensed. "But she is my life. I can't cut her out."

He felt something close to panic seize him. He didn't have answers, and he wanted them desperately. Then he heard himself saying something he never thought he would. "I like Hayley. And if she's around, it's okay. I can deal with it."

She moved back from his touch, hugging her arms around herself. "You can deal with it?"

"Look, I don't know what to say." He exhaled roughly with exasperation. "Correct me if I'm wrong, but this isn't complicated. It's simple. I want to see you. It's okay if Hayley is there. How much more simple can it get?"

He waited for her to answer, unease sliding up his spine the longer she stayed silent. Then she took a shaky breath. "I've never done this before," she said in a low voice. "I'm not sure if I can."

"Forget everything else. Don't let this be complicated. Just answer me one thing, do you want to?"

CHAPTER TEN

E.J. LITERALLY HELD his breath until Sara said, "We can be friends," in a voice so low that he barely heard the words. "That's all we can be."

"Friends?" he asked, the word almost foreign to him, at least when it came to women.

"That's all I can do," she whispered.

He stayed where he was. He wanted her as a friend, but he wanted so much more. "Why?"

"I just can't…I won't get into anything that I can't handle."

He moved closer again, but didn't touch her. "Why? Because you had a bad marriage?"

"It was more than that," she said, and he saw the pain in her eyes.

"It's over, isn't it?"

She nodded. "Yes. It's over."

"Then it's in the past." He ached to touch her again. "I'm not looking for some lifelong commitment. I told you that. And I like you. I want to get to know you. Can't we just take this a day at a time, and if it isn't right, that's it? We both walk away? No hard feelings?"

"That's okay for me," she said. "But Hayley, I just—"

"I like her," he said again. "I won't intrude on her, or make any promises. Okay?"

She hesitated, and he could literally see her weighing the options, figuring out what she was going to do. Then she said, "Okay, we can be friends, and see how that works."

That was enough for now. His phone rang and he answered. "Yes?"

"I'm back," Andrew said.

"I'll be right out," he said, putting the phone back in his pocket. "Okay, friends," he said to Sara, "and we'll see after that."

She nodded slightly. "We'll see," she whispered.

He hesitated, then touched her, cupping her chin in one hand, taking the time to skim his gaze over her face, taking in every gentle line and angle. Then he dipped his head and tasted her softly parted lips. There was no response from her, but she didn't push him away, either. That was a positive, he thought as he let her go.

"See you tomorrow?" he said, his voice low and raspy.

"Tomorrow," she echoed, then he reached for the door.

He opened the door, but before he could walk out into the early evening, Hayley was yelling "Edwood! Edwood!"

He turned, and she was running at him full tilt and he barely had time to reach out and scoop her off her feet to keep her from hitting him dead in the knees. When he had her in the air, she threw something at him. Thankfully, something soft. He watched a stuffed yellow elephant hit him in the chest and bounce to the floor. Sara scooped it up, and held it for him to see. "Mr. Bubba," she said, and her hand was less than steady, just about the way he felt right then.

Hayley snatched it out of her mother's hands, and she pushed it at E.J. "Bubba," she said.

"Nice," E.J. said as he looked at Sara. "Very nice." E.J. handed the girl to her mother. "I'll see you tomorrow?" he asked again.

"I'll be at work."

"Okay." Then he stepped out into the night, taking the sweetness of her taste with him. Tomorrow they'd really talk, he'd explain about his name, about who he was. He opened the back door of the limo and stepped in, startled when Martin spoke to him.

"I think we have a problem."

He hadn't expected his lawyer to be here, and as Andrew backed out of the driveway and headed home, E.J. sat forward and reached for a drink from the mini-bar. He poured a soda, asked Martin if he wanted one, then the two of them settled back with their drinks. "Okay, what's the problem?" E.J. asked before he took a sip.

"Well, there're two. Business and personal. Which one do you want first?"

"Just spill it, Martin."

"Okay, the papers can't be signed until Monday."

"That's fine," E.J. said, sipping his drink. "And the other problem?"

"Ray's insisting on coming down here."

He looked at Martin. "If you hadn't opened your mouth about Sara, he wouldn't be threatening to show up here, would he?"

Martin laughed. "Have you ever tried to sidestep that man's questions?"

"You're a highly paid attorney. If you can't evade his questions, what hope do the rest of us have?"

"True. He's all wound up about the ball."

E.J. finished the last of his drink. He'd been ready to pull out of the ball, to make his contribution and get out of town before it ever happened. But now he had an idea that maybe he'd go after all, especially since Sara was going to be there. "I'll talk to him and head him off."

"So, how's it going with your...friend?"

His friend. "Yes, my friend," he murmured. He filled his glass again and sat back. "Things are looking up."

TWO DAYS LATER THE PHONE in the office rang. Sara had come to the center with Hayley and Mary to take care of details for the ball, which was just one week away. Now, as she answered the call, she brushed her hair back from her face and slowly rotated her head to ease the tightness in her shoulders. "Just for Kids. How can I help you?"

"Hi, there," Edward said. "I was just checking on how you're doing."

He'd called twice yesterday, always asking how she was, saying he was busy, and that he hadn't forgotten about being her friend. That always made her smile. And when she heard his voice this time, the smile returned. "I'm really okay. Just a bit stiff. And then there's the stress over my car."

"Any word from the insurance company?"

"No, Mr. Row is having his accountant take care of everything instead."

There was an awkward silence, then he said, "I've been so tied up with business, but I have a break later on. Can we get together and talk?"

"I'm working straight through until six."

"Okay, six it is," he said, then hung up.

Mary came in right then and glanced at Sara putting the receiver back on the hook. "Anything important?" she asked.

"It was Edward just asking how I was doing after the accident?"

"Again? Very solicitous," Mary murmured, gathering up papers from the desk. "A good sign."

"Excuse me?" Sara asked as she looked across the desk at Mary.

"A man who worries about you is one who cares about your well-being, dear. Paul sounds as if he was very self-centered."

She didn't want to think about Paul. "Yes. He was."

"And Edward doesn't seem to be, does he?"

"Not really, but he's pretty sure about what he wants and what he doesn't want."

"Oh?" she asked. "Such as?"

"He doesn't want anything permanent,

and he really doesn't want to get involved with anyone with kids."

"And you believed him?"

"Why wouldn't I?"

Mary exhaled. "I've found, in my long life, that few people know what they really want until it is standing right in front of them." She started for the door, then stopped. "Oh, by the way, Marigold wants to see you out at the Sommers estate in about an hour. You can take my car. She wants to show you the room she thinks might work best for the kids."

Sara was glad to have the subject changed, and was really interested in seeing the Sommers estate. She'd heard everyone raving about the ballroom and the grounds and was anxious to see it for herself. "Okay, I'll head out there right away."

Mary reached in the pocket of her dress and tossed a set of keys onto the desk. "Car keys. Enjoy yourself."

At ten minutes to three, Sara was in Mary's car driving up to the main entrance to the Sommers estate. She came to two enormous wrought-iron gates set in stone columns that topped the gates by a good four feet. A keypad and speaker were set off from the left pillar, close to the drive. Sara rolled down her window, entered the numbers into the keypad and watched as the gates slowly parted.

She drove through, onto a wide cobbled drive that could have accommodated three cars side by side. It was lined by low-growing bushes that separated it from what seemed like acres and acres of rolling lawns, and dotted with old trees that laced together overhead. As she went up the drive, she crested a small rise, broke out of the trees and saw what she imagined was the main house, even if it looked ten times larger than any house she'd ever seen.

It was a sprawling structure, with high and low parts, some two stories, some single story, and one section that could have been three stories high. The roof was a thick adobe tile, the walls looked like textured stucco and brick, and the drive came to a stop in a huge circular area at the entry to the house, inlaid with bricks and tile.

In the center was a massive fountain and a twenty-foot-high portico that protected the double deeply carved doors.

She'd barely stopped by the sweep of inlaid tile stairs before a man dressed all in black appeared at the driver's window. He was narrow-faced, with thin blond hair, pale gray eyes and wearing a plainly tailored suit. There was great concern on his face. "What are you doing here?"

"I am here to see Marigold—"

He cut her off, saying, "And you were told to park at the service entrance, weren't you?"

"No, I don't think so."

"Well, you should have been told. No workpeople are supposed to come in the main entrance. Go to Service," he said, and motioned behind her. "Go back, take the side drive and park with the trucks."

"I'm sorry," she said.

He waved her words away with a sweep of one hand, and a sharp nod toward the way she'd just come. "Just park back there," he muttered.

She turned in the drive and followed the

road to a second entry. It was smaller, less impressive, but still intricate, with an overhang, a sweep of steps and party-planner trucks parked outside.

She parked Mary's car and headed for the entrance, carrying a briefcase filled with notes, plans and lists of needs for the kids' room. She started to knock on the door, but it was partially ajar, so she entered. She walked through an arch across from the door and came into a kitchen with stone floors, twelve-foot ceilings and appliances that could have been used to run a very large restaurant.

In the center, standing at a massive island, four people were bent over the granite counter, hard at work. A woman with brilliant red hair cut in a short bob, wearing all white, turned and smiled at Sara. "Hello again, Sara," she said, coming over to her.

"Hello."

"I'm glad you're here. I think I found the perfect room for the children to take over. It's actually a billiard room, and it usually contains three tables. But all of them are out for reconditioning and the owner gave us permission to use it."

"As long as there's lots of space and enough outlets for televisions, VCRs, video games?"

"There's actually a complete media center. I'd love for you to see it, but I need to finish up a few things first. So feel free to take a look on your own." Marigold carefully gave her directions. "You can't miss it. Let me know what else you'll need to make it work."

"Okay," Sara said. "I'll be back in a bit."

She stepped out of the kitchen into a broad, stone-floored hallway, but before the door to the kitchen closed, Marigold called out, "Oh, just a minute."

Sara turned, holding the door open. "What?"

"Stay on this side of the house. We gave our word that we wouldn't intrude in the west wing."

"How will I know if I've crossed the line?"

"The main entry is the demarcation line. Just don't go in it or past it. The upstairs is totally off-limits." She crinkled her nose and came closer, lowering her voice a bit. "The owner is in residence and we promised that he'd have his privacy."

"I've heard about him, but I didn't know he was living here."

"Probably came in for the ball. The staff said he's hardly ever here. Just stay clear, okay?"

"Absolutely," she said. "Although I might need a rescue party to find me if I get lost."

Marigold laughed. "Just leave a trail of bread crumbs," she said, then went back to the group in the kitchen.

Sara left, went past a series of closed doors, then stepped into a space that looked for all the world like a two-story rotunda. It was circular, probably thirty feet across, done with intricate wood and marble inlaid floors, with an arched doorway across to her left. To her right stood a set of twenty-foot-high doors, framed by ornate Roman pillars, and fashioned out of a deep, rich wood.

The famous ballroom, she thought, and crossed to the doors. One peek was all she wanted, just to see if it lived up to its billing. She heard voices and hammering as she eased back the right door and looked inside. She gasped in shock.

She'd imagined a big room, with crystal chandeliers and a polished floor. But she hadn't imagined anything like this. The room went beyond big. It was cavernous. The dimensions she'd read on the plans translated into a room so long that she thought a football team could play in there and still have room for bleachers. Workmen at the far end were assembling what looked like a stage, and seemed very far away. Almost as wide as it was long, it was topped by a ceiling that was a massive version of the entry dome. It soared higher and was inlaid with murals and gilt, a ceiling that she thought had been designed to imitate the Sistine Chapel, elegant and overdone, yet stunningly beautiful.

She could barely comprehend the single chandelier hanging from the center of the dome. It had to be twenty feet across, all crystal and shimmer, and probably ten feet deep. The floors were dark marble and polished wood, all of which shone to perfection.

Mary hadn't been exaggerating just how much room they'd have. This was conspicuous consumption at its best, Sara thought, and moved back, closing the door quietly.

The ball was going to be spectacular.

She made her way to the billiard room, but when she tugged on the door, she discovered it was locked. She thought Marigold had said the second door. Sara looked back. Maybe she'd said the third door? She tried, but it was locked, too. Then she saw the entry, a space that was even more ostentatious than the ballroom entry.

Looking at her surroundings in awe, Sara suddenly heard footsteps on the stairs. She looked up and was stunned to see Edward approaching, closely reading a piece of paper as he descended. In jeans, a plain white T-shirt and boots, he looked as casual as always, but what was he doing on E. J. Sommers's staircase?

"Edward!" she gasped, hurrying over to the foot of the staircase, and looked up at him. "What are you doing here?"

He stopped when he saw her, his eyes widened, his shock as great as hers. She hurried up three steps to reach for his hand. "We are not supposed to be in this part of the house. That Marigold lady said under no circumstance were we to be over here, and you were…" She looked past him at the elegant staircase. "Good grief, were you up there? That's really off-limits."

While she talked, she was tugging at him, trying to get him to go with her, but he stood still, not moving at all. She might as well have been a fly buzzing around him for all the momentum she had trying to get him out of there. "Please," she begged, tugging at his hand. He finally went down the last steps to the entry floor. "We have to get out of here," she said.

"Sara, stop," he said in a low voice as he held on to her tightly. "I thought I'd see you at six and—"

"Edward, listen to me. No one is supposed to be in this part of the house."

"I know," he said, but he didn't make a move to get out of there.

Then she heard someone behind them,

footsteps tapping on the hard floors, foot-steps that got faster, then were behind her in the entry. "Sara," Marigold was saying as she came closer. "I heard a voice, and couldn't believe you were in here. I told you not to—" As Sara turned, her hand still caught by Edward's, she saw Mari-gold, but she wasn't looking at her. She was staring at Edward.

"We were just going back to the billiard room," Sara said, and frowned at Edward. "Weren't we?"

"No, we weren't, Sara," he said.

"The billiard room," she said, motioning with her head to the hallway she'd stepped out of. "Help me find it?"

"Mr. Sommers, I don't know what to say." Then Marigold had Sara by her arm. "I came to make sure Sara found your bil-liard room. I thought she might get lost, but I didn't know she'd come in here."

They were talking over Sara, and it took her a very long moment to realize what Marigold had called Edward. She thought he was Mr. Sommers? That didn't make sense, not until Sara looked back at Edward. He wasn't correcting her at all. Then it hit her. "You're E. J. Sommers?" she breathed.

"Of course he is," Marigold said. "And he's made it very clear that he doesn't want workpeople in this part of his house.

His house? She jerked her hand back from her hold on him, almost stumbling into Marigold, who was still trying to get her out of there. She stared at Edward, her stomach in such knots that she thought she might be sick.

"Sara?" Edward said, coming toward her. He reached out a hand and she struck out, not just slapping him, but punching his hand before she realized what she was doing. Marigold gasped, but Edward didn't do anything more than pull his hand back and take a deep breath before he said, "We need to talk."

She couldn't imagine what kind of a game he thought he was playing with her. Was it because he was just plain bored, that he thought he'd do something different and pretend to be a worker? And she'd bought into it. She'd started to… She swallowed hard at the impact of her next thought. She'd started to care, to let her defenses down, to allow herself to have a flicker of hope that something could happen between them.

"No," she said, and turned, hurrying across the entry, making her escape. She heard footsteps behind her, and she reached for the first door she came to. Locked. Then saw a door she'd missed before, set back in a shallow alcove, and she tried it. It opened and she all but fell inside, closing it behind her.

She looked up and knew she'd finally found the billiard room. Like the other rooms, it was impressive. But most important of all, it was empty. Totally empty.

She stood just inside the door, hugging her arms around herself, trying to breathe, but finding it difficult. She closed her eyes tightly, fighting the urge to scream in rage. A rage directed at herself as much as at Edward. Paul had been a fast talker, making her believe everything he said and lying through his teeth. "I'm working every night," he'd told her, and had gone into great detail about the "gigs" he'd been playing on the road, keeping him away from her and Hayley for months at a time. The truth was, he'd been working some, but playing a whole lot more.

"You're the only one for me," he told her with such heartfelt sincerity that she'd believed him. She guessed that the women he'd "played" with on the road didn't count. They were amusement. "Family is important to me," he'd said at one point. And then he left.

"Lies, lies, lies," she muttered as she opened her eyes and wondered if she had a mark on her forehead that let men know she was an easy target.

The door opened, knocking into her back, and she lurched forward, then turned and saw Edward coming into the room. Before she could do anything, he'd closed the door and leaned back against it. She was trapped, and that made her want to scream all over again. "Go away," she managed to say around the tightness in her throat.

"No." He didn't move.

"Edward…E.J… Eddy…Ed." She shook

her head. "I don't even know what to call you."

"Edward. That's my name."

"Sure."

"Edward Jonathan Sommers. Edward is fine."

"Whatever," she said, and ducked her head, going around him to make a grab for the door handle. Even though the room was huge, she was suffocating.

Her hand touched the cold handle at the same time Edward caught her by her shoulders and pulled her around to face him. She struggled and hit at his hand on her. She'd never struck anyone in her life, and she'd hit him twice in less than five minutes. She hated herself for that, and hated him for driving her to it. "Let me go!" she ground out, pushing with one hand against his chest.

He did, but so abruptly that she stumbled backward, steadying herself against the wall. His hazel eyes were intense.

"Let me explain," he said, "then you can leave if you want to."

She hugged her arms around herself

again, trying to control the trembling. "No, I don't want to hear anything." Her eyes were burning and she was terrified that she'd start to cry. "I just want to go."

"Sara, please," he said softly. "Five minutes. That's it."

He was still between her and the door and she wasn't about to push him away or try to squeeze past him. Five minutes. But she wouldn't believe a thing he said. "Sure, go ahead, I know the drill," she muttered.

"What drill?"

She threw her hands out to either side, and hated the burning at the back of her eyes. "I'm sorry, but you've got it all wrong. Or the ever popular, I didn't mean it, and it won't happen again. But it does." Her hands were curled into tight fists now. "Over and over and over and over again."

He had her by her shoulders and she froze. "Hey, we were supposed to be talking about me, not you or your ex."

"Don't touch me," she muttered tightly.

"Sara, you have to understand," he said.

"Oh, now that was one of Paul's favorites, right before he told me more lies."

"I'm sorry that he did that, but I'm not Paul."

She blinked rapidly, hoping against hope that there wouldn't be tears. She couldn't bear that, crying again in front of this man. She wouldn't. "I left him because…" She bit her lip hard. No, she wasn't going to tell him all of that. "Forget it."

His eyes narrowed on her. "Just hear me out and know that it's the truth."

She didn't have a choice. "Just say it," she said, and prepared herself for a truth she didn't want to hear, and a pain she knew would only get worse.

CHAPTER ELEVEN

SARA FELT HIS fingers pressing into her shoulders, hovering just this side of real pain, but she didn't move. In some odd way it helped her focus. "Okay, I'll make this simple," Edward said. "I'm Edward Jonathan Sommers—E.J. to a lot of people, Edward to some—and I've got a bit of money."

"I've heard that," she muttered.

"I know, you've heard a lot about me. I remember." He exhaled with a sharp shake of his head. "My life isn't what the public thinks. What they don't understand is I have people lie to me all the time. They tell me I'm wonderful when they think I'm a jerk, or they say I'm brilliant when they think I'm as dumb as dirt. My accountant got this place for me as a write-off, and you know what? I haven't even seen most of the rooms."

He let her go, stepping back half a pace, but still facing her. "To be blunt, I'm wealthy and that gives me a degree of power. That makes me a target, and when I meet people, they see what I am, instead of who I am. And women tend to be more blinded by the *what* than the *who*. So when I met you, and you didn't know who I was, we dealt with each other on an even field, which was very refreshing."

"So, you thought if I knew who you were I'd go after you for your money?"

"Actually, yes, I did."

"I think I should be offended," she murmured.

"I didn't know you, but I started to like the idea of just being me, and remembering how I used to be before I stumbled into this life I have now."

"And I'm supposed to feel sorry for you?" she asked.

"No, not at all. I've been very lucky, and I know it, but my life is too complicated." He tucked the tips of his fingers into his jeans pockets. "At the moment, I'm selling off part of EJS Corporation to Lyn-Tech. Streamlining things. Getting out from under the world I've created for myself. I've decided that this is going next." He motioned around the room. "I never wanted it and sure don't need it."

Sara watched Edward, and hated the fact that she was very close to believing him. She could see something in him, a sense of isolation that was almost painful to watch. "So you pretended to be someone working at LynTech because...?"

"You thought that's who I was, and I decided to keep it that way for a while, to see how you might feel about me." He rocked forward on the balls of his feet. "Do you understand what I'm trying to say?"

She did, and that scared her. "I think so."

"The reason I was going to see you at six was so that I could tell you about myself."

"Finally?"

"I was going to tell you when we met after work at the center when you first started working there."

"Then why didn't you?"

"Things changed." He shrugged. "It didn't seem important."

She understood. "You saw Hayley." That brought everything into perspective. Hayley. "No kids. No affinity for kids. I remember. You made that very clear."

E.J. hated having his words thrown back at him like that. He'd meant them when he said them, but now he wasn't entirely sure how he felt about Hayley. She had that smile like Sara's and the eyes. "I'm not a kid person. I never have been. But why can't I just be her friend? Someone she can throw toys at."

He'd hoped she'd laugh, but she didn't. "To get anything thrown at you, you'd have to get close enough to be hit, and that might be hard on you."

"I can take it," he said. "I'll buy a catcher's mitt."

"Why are you doing this?" she asked.

"I want to see you, and Hayley is part of the package. You've made that very clear."

"Have you done this with any of…any other women?" She smiled slightly, but it was a brittle expression that he didn't like at all. "I heard you dated. Surely one of them had children?"

His reputation preceded him again. "Oh, Sara, I've dated, maybe more than most, I don't know. You were married. We both have baggage. But it's what's right now that counts. And right now, all I can do is promise you that I will never do anything to hurt Hayley in any way. I'm not her father, but I'd like to be her friend."

She stared at him hard. "It's easy to make promises," she murmured.

"I mean to keep this one," he said, and came closer to her, leaving just inches separating them. "I'm sorry that you've gone through what you did with your ex-husband, that you had to leave, and that you put up these barriers to protect yourself. I hate him for doing that to you." He reached out, his hands resting on her shoulders, her heat seeping through her shirt. "But I'm not him. You have to see that. I wasn't lying to hurt you or manipulate you. I'm not him. Trust me, and give me a chance?"

He saw her take a breath, saw the way her shoulders trembled slightly, and he could see a war going on inside her. He knew he was asking her to make a huge leap of faith, and he wanted to be there to catch her. "Okay," she finally whispered. "We'll start over again."

E.J. felt relief flood through him, leaving him light-headed. "Are you sure?" he breathed.

Her tongue darted out to touch her full bottom lip, then Sara whispered, "Yes, but…no more lies. Never. No matter what. I can't deal with lies." A single tear silently slipped from the corner of one eye, but she made no move to brush it away.

"No more lies," he said. "I promise." He drew her to him, enfolding her in his arms and relishing the feel of her against him. He exhaled with relief, feeling as if he'd just fought a battle and come out the winner. "Where do we start?" he finally asked.

She eased back and out of his hold. "I don't know," she said softly.

Neither did he. He cupped her chin, tipping her head up to look in her eyes. "We'll play it by ear?"

"Yes, I guess so. For now, I have to get

to work. Marigold was—" Her eyes widened. "Oh, no, Marigold!" Color dotted her cheeks. "She saw me hit you."

"You actually punched me, but I'm fine."

"I can't begin to think what Marigold must think is going on."

"She'll think we had a friendly disagreement."

"Oh, sure she will," she muttered. "All she thinks is that I hit E. J. Sommers."

"And your point is?"

She shook her head. "You and me… She'll be thinking… I mean, it couldn't have looked worse."

E.J. thought it could have looked a lot worse if Marigold had walked in on him doing what he wanted to do at that moment. A knock sounded, and E.J. stared at Sara for a long moment, tamping down that instant response he felt when she was close, then he turned and reached to open the door. Marigold stood there looking a bit tentative. "I didn't know whether or not you were finished in here."

"We were just trying to figure things out," he said, looking back at Sara.

"Is everything okay?" Marigold asked.

"I think so," Sara said, and moved away from E.J. "It's a great room, but the floors are so hard. We have some sleeping bags and nap mats. I just don't know if they'll be soft enough." She was looking around the room speculatively, as though nothing had happened. "I don't know if it would work for sleeping."

"Good point," Marigold said, crouching and touching the wooden floor.

Sara crossed to the media wall where all of the connections for televisions and music were set up in a single panel close to the floor. She crouched in front of it, and reached out, touching a bank of at least a dozen electrical plugs. "This would be great for the TVs and video equipment. Everything's in the garage now."

"The room's fully wired for media connections," E.J. said.

She stood and turned, looking around the room. "We've got two televisions, one from the center, and one from Mary. We have two video-game consoles, some board games, two popcorn makers, and then there's the pizza." She paused. "The parents are supplying sleeping rolls and blankets for their own children, but there are several kids who might come up short on the sleeping supplies.

"What I need to see is how we can use the kitchen for the food without intruding on the ball preparations and the guests," she said to Marigold, as if E.J. wasn't even there.

"Why not use one of the smaller kitchens so that you won't get in anyone's way?" he asked.

"A smaller kitchen?" Sara finally looked at him.

"Across the entry in the great room, there's a bar, and behind it is a working kitchen. You can use it. Just call my housekeeper, Mrs. Stroud, and she'll get it set up for you."

"You don't have to—" Sara started to say, but he cut her off.

"No, I don't, but I want to," he said.

"Thank you, Mr. Sommers," Marigold said.

E.J. looked at Sara and felt that the wall

between them was firmly back in place. Could he break down that wall for good? "No problem," he said to Marigold.

Marigold opened the door again, ready to leave, and Sara headed over to go with her. "Sara?" E.J. said before she could disappear into the hallway.

She glanced back at him, her eyes shadowed. "Yes?"

He stared at her, unsure what to say. Certainly he wasn't going to beg her to go out with him. "I meant to ask if you're okay after the accident?"

"I've already told you that I am."

"Has the attorney contacted you yet?"

"No, not yet."

E.J. wondered why the man would use his attorney for something this cut-and-dried. "Okay. Well, see you later?"

Sara nodded, at least he thought she did, but the motion was very slight. And then she was gone. E.J. left the room and headed toward his quarters. When he stepped into the sitting area of his suite, he crossed to the house phone and called the housekeeper, Mrs. Stroud.

"Yes, sir?" she answered after two rings.

"The people from the ball need things to help put the party together. I want you to offer to help them in any way possible."

"Oh, yes, sir. Of course. It's a wonderful cause."

"Also, in the billiard room, get everything set up. Get some extra video-game consoles, games for them, and any other toys you think might be fun for kids that range in age from two or so to young teens."

She listened silently and he realized she was making a list. "Yes, sir."

He remembered Hayley's penchant for throwing things. "Get some stuffed animals, too. We need rugs in there. Soft rugs to cover the floor. Take them from other rooms if you have to, but get the floor covered as much as possible."

"Is that it, sir?"

"Sleeping bags. Get some of those, too, child size. That's all I can think of, but if you come up with anything else you think children need or like, go ahead and get it."

"Yes, sir."

He hung up, then hit the extension for Andrew, his driver, and asked for the car to be brought around to the side entrance by the terrace in ten minutes. After he hung up, he reached for his leather jacket on a nearby chair, and as he shrugged into it, his cell phone rang. He saw Martin's number and answered as he strode out of the suite, heading toward the stairs.

"It's me. What's wrong now?" he asked.

"Just an update." After the original problem with the deal, things had gone smoothly. Until yesterday. Instead of seeing Sara, as he'd planned, he'd had to deal with a business associate who shouldn't have known anything about the LynTech deal. The man had made him an offer that topped LynTech's just enough to get his attention. He'd refused, then called Martin to find out what was going on.

Now Martin was saying, "We don't know who leaked the information, but Zane wanted me to assure you that he had no part in it. He's got his end under control, and he hopes that things will go ahead as planned."

Since dealing with Zane Holden, one of LynTech's CEOs, E.J. was certain of one thing—Holden was a man of his word. "Absolutely. If he says it's under control, I'll take his word for it."

"That was my reaction. He's contacting someone he knows in corporate security to take over an investigation, a man he trusts completely. It's not just our deal that's been leaking, it's other confidential information that could end up damaging LynTech if it's not stopped." He took a breath. "So, rest assured, all's right with the world."

"Okay, if you're satisfied, I am, too," he said, stopping at the bottom of the stairs. He was ready to leave, but he didn't. Instead, he headed back to the main kitchen. "Martin, I need you to check on an accident that happened a few days ago." He gave him all the information and what he knew about the man who'd caused it. "It's being settled by the man's attorney for some reason, and I want to know why."

"Why are you getting involved?"

"Call it a gut reaction. I just need it checked out."

"I've learned to trust your gut reactions," Martin said on a laugh. "Give me a bit and I'll get back to you.

"I'm heading over to LynTech, so catch up with me there."

E.J. approached the open kitchen door as he put away his phone, and looked inside the room. Sara was sitting on a high stool at a central island with Marigold, going over what looked like floor plans. Both women were intent on the papers in front of them and didn't hear him until he was standing beside them. "Sara?" he said.

Sara jumped and turned to him. "Oh, I didn't know you were there."

He watched her, remembering the way it felt to kiss her, and he couldn't think of what to say. "I was just…" Just what? Thinking that he wanted to take her away, to be alone with her? "I just wanted to make sure things are okay now."

Marigold touched Sara's arm. "I'll be right back. I need to get the layout for the parking." She headed out of the kitchen.

E.J. stepped closer to Sara. "Is everything okay with us?"

"It's fine," she answered in a low voice, darting a look at the other people in the room.

"Then let's do dinner tonight."

"No."

"Sara, why not?"

Color touched her cheeks faintly. "I need to think about things first," she said.

"Why?"

She took a breath and he could have sworn it was a bit shaky. "Because…"

She looked at the others in the room once again, then motioned him to the door. Together they stepped outside. "I can't just casually go out or do anything. I made an awful mistake with Paul, and Hayley's the only good that came of it."

"I know all of this. It doesn't explain why you're so dead set against letting anyone get close to you. I thought we'd made progress today."

"I said we could start all over again, that doesn't mean I'm willing to jump into something without looking."

"It's dinner, just dinner." His frustration was showing and he knew it. He couldn't

help it. "What was all of that about before, you agreeing to trust me, to give me
a chance? Is this a game or what?"

Her expression tightened, and when she
spoke her voice was low and tense. "This
is no game. Do you know why I really left
Chicago?"

He shook his head. "Why?"

"Because Paul would come back. He'd
show up, and Hayley and I wouldn't be
safe."

His stomach knotted. "He abused you?"
he asked tightly.

"No, no, not like that. Never. But he
took everything I had, everything I was
or could be. He kept taking and taking and
taking, and I knew if I stayed there, Hayley and I would never be able to make a
life. And she wouldn't be safe. I had to
get away from him, as far as I could, and
Houston was the only far-off place where
I knew anyone."

"What does that have to do with us?"

She clenched her hands into fists at her
sides, and he could see the tension building in her. "I make awful choices. Don't

you understand? I think things are okay, but they aren't. I trust people I shouldn't. I can't..." Her lip was unsteady and he saw the brightness in her eyes. "I can't even trust myself."

"He did quite a number on you, didn't he?"

"I did it all myself," she said.

"No, you didn't," he muttered, and understood a bit more of what made Sara Flynn tick. The man she'd married had made her doubt everything, and she couldn't figure out what to do or what not to do. "You're still letting him control you, even though he's not around. You can't break out of that cycle, can you?"

"It's not that simple, Edward," she said.

"I think it is. You either trust yourself or you don't. You can trust me, or you can't. It's your choice, Sara."

She clasped her hands tightly in front of herself and shook her head. "You don't understand," she breathed, and moved past him, going back inside the house.

"Oh, yes, I do," he whispered, then turned and left.

SARA GOT BACK TO THE CENTER just before six and barely got inside before Hayley came running over to her, squealing at the top of her lungs. Then she saw another little girl who had come in on the weekend, running after Hayley. "She gotted my fish!" the girl exclaimed when she saw Sara picking up her daughter.

"Your fish?" She looked at her daughter and saw she was holding a box of crackers that were baked in the shape of fishes. "Oh, Hayley, you took her snack," she said.

Hayley hugged the box tightly to her as if it were a rare jewel. "Mine!" she pronounced.

"No, they're hers," Sara said, and took the box away from her daughter, then gave it to the other child. "Sorry."

"Thanks," the girl said, and ran off… fast.

Hayley's bottom lip was sticking out in a pout. "Mine," she said in a low voice.

"No, not yours," she said.

Mary stood there, smiling. "I tried to stop her, but she's fast. She had those crackers before I could get to her."

"She is fast," she said as Hayley wiggled free and darted off toward the tree as soon as her feet hit the ground.

"So, how did it go at the house?" Mary asked.

Sara exhaled. "Crazy," she said.

Mary motioned to the quiet room. "Come and talk," she said.

They went into the quiet room, and Mary took the old rocking chair. Sara dropped down in one of the huge beanbags on the floor. She stretched out, her hands over her head, her feet out in front of her. "Boy, it feels good to sit down," she said.

"So, why was it so crazy at the estate?" Mary asked.

Although Sara had no intentions of telling Mary about Edward, she found herself doing just that. When she stopped, she leaned forward, crossed her legs and buried her face in her hands. "I am so stupid," she muttered.

"Why, because you didn't know who he was?"

That should be why, but it wasn't. "Partly," she admitted.

"And the other part?"

"I don't know," she whispered.

"Are you sure?"

She looked up at Mary. "Mary, for once I actually thought that maybe I'd found someone who was what he claimed. And maybe I was letting myself believe that... well, that maybe I wasn't so stupid when it came to men after all."

"And him turning out to be E. J. Sommers makes him...what?"

"E. J. Sommers," she said.

"And that means?"

"Oh, I don't know," she said, and fell backward into the seat.

"Sara, you're young and beautiful and you've got your whole life ahead of you. Don't throw it away."

She sat up. "I'm not."

"And what if you are?"

"What if I mess things up again, and this time Hayley gets hurt? He told me he doesn't like kids. He isn't talking about anything more than...just...well, you know, getting to know each other, and seeing where things go."

"I might be older, but I do remember what the man-woman thing is all about, dear."

"Okay, then you know that I can't just let it go and see what happens."

"That's your option, dear."

"I can't let Hayley get involved when it's all so tentative with Edward. All the 'maybes' and the 'what-ifs' just leave me feeling unsteady. And he's got this life and the people in it, and…" She bit her lip. "It's all so scary."

"It could be. You know, I have to say I've heard things about him and the women he's dated, but I also think that most of it's just copy for the tabloids." She smiled. "My dear, if he was half as active as they say he is, he'd be worn out by now."

Sara couldn't smile, but she nodded. "He told me that what people think of him and what's true isn't necessarily the same thing."

"See, I told you. And from what Robert's said about him, he thinks he's an honorable man." She exhaled. "Just remember that sometimes what you really want turns out to be different from what you think you want."

"If you say so," she said on a sigh.

A knock sounded softly on the door, and Mary called, "Come on in."

Robert Lewis came into the room. "Mary, I was looking for you," he said.

Sara got up, sensing that she wasn't needed here. "I'd better go out and see what damage Hayley's done this time," she said.

"Okay, dear," Mary said.

Mr. Lewis smiled at her. "Good to see you again."

"Yes, sir," Sara said, ducking out of the room and closing the door behind her. The way those two had looked at each other... there was definitely something going on. She shook her head, a bit shocked that she found herself jealous that the older woman could be so open to things. She hadn't been able to be that way since Paul had fallen into her life. And for that, she hated him. Really hated him. Maybe he would cost her everything. She'd thought he had before, but maybe she'd been wrong. Maybe

Edward was right—her ex could ruin her life without even being in the same city.

For the next three days, Sara waited for something to happen, but nothing did. She worked on the ball, and on Tuesday she went in to work and no one mentioned E. J. Sommers. If he was at LynTech, he never came near the center or the café. If he was at his house when she went there late Monday afternoon, he stayed out of sight. She started to think that she'd driven him away. Maybe she'd gone too far, and he was no longer interested. That left her feeling empty and angry.

With four days until the ball, she worked nonstop, going from the café, to the center, to the estate. Her life seemed to be a blur, but it kept her from thinking about Edward and what she might have thrown away. She'd just about decided that it had all been an illusion, that a man like E. J. Sommers would never fit into her world, that he'd obviously had second thoughts about starting over, or being friends.

She got to the estate at four o'clock on

Thursday and almost ran into Marigold as she was going in the service entrance.

"You won't believe this," the woman said, reversing her direction and grabbing Sara by her hand, all but dragging her through the kitchen. "Just wait until you see this. It's just…it's awesome," she gushed as they walked down the hall. She stopped by the billiard room, threw the door open dramatically and said, "Tah-dah!"

Sara stepped into the room and stopped dead in her tracks. Where the room had once been skimpily filled with their donations, now it was transformed into a child's paradise. Deep green carpeting covered the entire floor, and three large-screen TVs lined one wall, along with VCRs, DVD players, video consoles. A bookshelf was filled with tapes and DVDs. In the center was an air hockey table, and beyond that were a dozen pup tents set up in three circles. On the wall was a mound of stuffed toys that almost blocked one of the windows.

"Where did this all come from?" she asked, stunned.

"Mr. Sommers."

CHAPTER TWELVE

SARA SPUN AROUND. "Edward donated all of this?"

Marigold nodded with a huge grin. "What a guy, huh? They're to be used for the ball, then donated to the hospital for the children's wing."

"Oh, my," she breathed, slipping off her sandals. Sara was stunned. The man had provided everything the children could possibly want.

"Sara, I think we have you to thank for the whole thing."

"Me?"

"Oh, come on. I could see what was going on between the two of you." Her grin deepened. "Honey, when you're crazy about someone, it shows, even when you try to hide it."

"No, no, no, no, no," she said, shaking her head.

"Go tell that to someone who believes you."

"Marigold," she began, then stopped herself. What did it matter now that he'd gone away? "He's just trying to help."

"And trying to impress you in the process, I'd say."

"Marigold, it's a tax write-off. That's all it is to Mr. Sommers."

"That's all *what* is to me?"

Sara turned and felt the breath leave her body. Edward. Strolling in wearing jeans, a T-shirt and boots. His hair looked damp, as if he'd just gotten out of a shower, and it was obvious he'd just shaved. She drew air into her lungs and watched him come closer.

E.J. heard her voice first, then saw her as he stepped into the billiard room. Sara. In jeans, a white top and bare feet. And even though he'd begun to think that whatever had started between them was over, it wasn't. He knew that the instant he heard her...and saw her.

He'd gone back to Dallas to think and to get some space so he could put things with Sara in perspective. He'd almost fallen into a relationship with her when he knew what she expected. Things he couldn't possibly give her. Marriage? No. A father for her child? No. And she wasn't about to give him her trust. That was obvious. So, he'd left, and taken time, lots of time, with empty days and empty nights. He'd thought that his sanity had been restored, until he saw her again. He was wrong, very wrong. "So?" he asked. "What is it to me?"

"Nothing," Sara said quickly. "Marigold was just saying that this was all great. I was agreeing."

She hadn't been, but he wasn't going to push anything. "Mrs. Stroud did a good job picking things out?"

"She did a fantastic job," Marigold said.

E.J. walked farther into the room, stopping just in front of Sara and taking time to look around while he figured out why he'd come here in the first place. "Yes, she did."

Then he met Sara's gaze, and the jolt of connection shot through him. And he knew he couldn't just walk away and let it go. "So, how are you doing?" he asked.

She shifted nervously and shrugged. "Fine. Busy."

"How's Hayley?" he found himself asking, and was a bit surprised that he really wanted to know.

"She's fine. She loves the center."

He motioned to the mound of stuffed toys. "I told Mrs. Stroud to make sure there were plenty of soft toys, given her penchant for throwing things."

He'd hoped she'd smile, but she didn't. She said, "Good idea," then went around him toward the door.

"Sara?" he said.

She stopped and turned. "Yes?"

"I need to talk to you privately."

She started to shake her head, then Marigold said, "Okay, I can take a hint. You two talk. I've got things to do."

Sara looked at the party planner as if she'd suggested murder. "No, you don't have to—"

"That's okay, no problem," the other

woman said, and left the room, closing the door behind her.

Now it was just the two of them. Sara stood very still, less than five feet from him, staring at the floor. "Don't look as if you're about to be tortured," he said.

She looked at him. "I thought you'd left."

"I did," he admitted. "I went to Dallas and did what I had to do there, then this morning, I flew back. I didn't know you were here." He hadn't known, but part of him had hoped she would be. "I heard your voice from the hallway."

She fidgeted nervously with the tail of her shirt, twisting it around and around on her forefingers. "Why did you do this?"

"Do what? Come in here when I heard your voice?"

"No, this," she said, sweeping her hand to the room at large. "All of this."

"Charity," he said.

"Sure, a tax write-off. That's a given. But this is more than necessary. This is overkill."

She was right. Total overkill. "Okay, I went overboard...a bit."

"A bit?"

Was that the suggestion of a smile? He sure hoped so. He had missed that smile. "Okay, more than a bit. But it was for a good cause, wasn't it?"

She was silent for a long moment, then finally exhaled. "Yes, it's a good cause, and no matter why you did it, the kids will be thrilled."

He felt as if a knot inside him had just unraveled and he could breathe a little easier. "I hope so. And how about you, are you happy with it?"

Then she smiled. A real smile. She nodded and her lips turned up just a bit at the corners. "How could I not be happy with what you've donated?" she breathed.

"Good. Very good," he murmured.

She eyed him narrowly. "Why did you do it?"

He shrugged. "Maybe it was to see you smile, and it worked, didn't it?"

Wrong thing to say. The smile was gone again. "Edward, if you did this to impress me, it worked. Now I have to get back to work. We're going crazy getting everything ready for Saturday night."

He went closer to her, not about to let their moment together end before it had truly begun. "It's…" He glanced at his watch. "It's getting late and the workday is almost over."

She tensed. She knew what he was going to say before he said it, and she was already forming her rejection. But before she could say anything, the door opened and Mary stood there holding Hayley. "Oh, good, I found you," she said, smiling at Sara.

Hayley lunged toward her mother, into her arms, and hugged Sara around the neck. "What's going on?" Sara asked, automatically starting to rock Hayley slightly.

"Hayley wanted Mommy, and the others left earlier than usual, so I got a taxi and brought her out to find you." She glanced at the room, then really looked at it. "Goodness gracious, this is beyond anything I imagined!" She all but clapped her hands with joy. "It's tremendous."

Hayley squirmed, so Sara let her down. She made a beeline for the stuffed animals, literally throwing herself into the mountain and giggling. Mary turned to Edward. "You did this, didn't you?"

"My housekeeper did," he admitted.

Mary made her way toward him and hugged him tightly. "You doll. You absolute doll!" She looked at Sara. "What a lucky day when you dropped that tray in the café. Look at what it did for us!"

Sara didn't look convinced, but she nodded. "I was just thanking Edward," she said.

"And I'm adding my thanks," Mary said.

The door opened and Robert Lewis walked in. He spotted Mary first and smiled. "Found you, finally," he said, then saw E.J. and Sara. He came over to them, his hand extended to E.J. "Well, imagine finding you here. I thought you were back in Dallas until the ball?"

E.J. noticed the way Robert got close to Mary and she laid a hand on his arm. "That was the plan, then something came up," he said.

"Good to have you back," Robert murmured. Then he glanced at Sara. "You're doing a wonderful job on this."

"Thanks," she said.

Hayley ran back to the adults holding a big fluffy ball in both her hands. She looked from person to person, then turned to E.J. "Ball," she said, and he knew what was coming. He got his hands up just in time to catch the ball before it hit his midsection.

"Got it," he said, and tossed it back to her. He looked at Robert. "You've got to be fast around her."

"You're up to it," Robert said with a smile, then turned to Mary. "Ready to leave?"

She nodded. "Sara, use my car to get home and I'll get it tomorrow. Is it okay to leave Hayley here with you?"

"It's just fine. She can test the toys."

"Good idea," Mary said, then called to Hayley. "Bye, bye."

Hayley wiggled a hand at her and climbed into the stuffed-animal pile looking for another missile to launch at some unsuspecting target. Then Mary looked at

E.J. "I have an idea. Why don't the three of you come to dinner with us?"

E.J. didn't miss the look on Robert's face. The man had obviously planned on having dinner alone with Mary. But this would be a good way to get to know Sara better. "That's up to Sara."

"I have to do a lot more here. I couldn't leave for at least an hour."

"Well, that's too long for me," Robert said quickly. "I'm starving."

Mary looked disappointed. "Oh, what a shame."

"Maybe another time," Robert said, and took Mary by her arm. "We need to get going."

"Of course, Robert, but I need to talk to Edward for a moment," she said, and together they left the room. "He'll be right back," she called to Sara over her shoulder just before she closed the door.

Robert stood silently by Mary as she faced E.J. She didn't look happy. "I don't know what's going on, or why you didn't tell Sara who you really were before she accidentally found out, but the first time you took her home, I told you that she was vulnerable, and that she's had a very bad time."

"She's told me about her past."

"Probably as little as she could. But let me fill you in a bit. Her husband drained her dry in every way he could, with other women, money, but especially emotionally. She's gone through the mill, and she needs good things to happen to her now." She studied him again. "I'd hate to see her hurt."

"So would I," he murmured.

Robert spoke for the first time. "Mary, I think he understands." His blue eyes held E.J.'s gaze. "Don't you?"

"Yes, sir, I do," he said, then smiled at Mary to break the tension. "Is this where you ask me what my intentions are toward Sara?"

"I wasn't going to," she said soberly. "But since you mentioned it, what are your intentions toward Sara?"

When he'd left Houston a few days ago, his intentions had been to let it go. Let her go. But the minute he saw her again, he knew he couldn't. Sara was worth fighting for, he'd do whatever it took to make her happy. "I want her to be happy, and to feel safe."

"And Hayley?"

He rubbed a hand around the back of his neck. "The same thing," he said, and knew it was true. "I want her to be safe and happy."

Mary nodded, obviously approving. "Okay, we're going to dinner. Have a lovely evening," she said, and left arm in arm with Robert.

E.J. stayed where he was for a moment, amazed at what he'd just told Mary. But everything he'd said was true. Maybe he wasn't looking for marriage or a family, but he wanted Sara and Hayley to be safe and happy. As he walked through the door that would lead him back to Sara, he felt very much like a moth drawn to a flame.

"Too bad we didn't go to dinner with those two," E.J. said as he approached Sara. "It might have been fun to see Robert putting the moves on Mary."

Sara watched Edward coming closer,

and knew that whatever Mary had wanted with him had gone okay. He looked relaxed and he was joking. "Oh, that's awful."

"Why? They're both adults," he said with an easy smile.

"Well, sure, of course they are, and I kind of thought the same thing, but Mary's never said much about it to me. They were close, years ago. And they finally caught up with each other." She shrugged. "Who knows?"

"Stranger things have happened, I guess."

"I guess so," Sara said, and felt that the room, despite being huge, suddenly seemed very small.

"So, you have work to do?"

She knew she did, but, for the life of her, she couldn't remember what any of that work was. Ever since Edward had walked back into her world after being gone only a few days, she hadn't been able to gather her thoughts. Now, as Edward stood there watching her, Sara realized she was waiting for his next move. "Yes, I do."

"How much work?"

"Tons."

"How does that translate into real time?" he asked.

"Like I said, at least an hour, if not longer."

"Okay, then, I'd better let you get back to it," he said as he walked to the door. Just like that, he was leaving. He looked back at her. "If I were you, I'd get those wooden blocks and hide them from Hayley. Or be careful and practice ducking," he said with a boyish grin, then he was gone.

Sara stared at the door and realized how disappointed she was. Anticipation had been growing in her from that first moment she saw him come into the room, mingling with a relief that he hadn't just walked away. It wasn't rational, and neither was this crushing disappointment that he was gone again.

She felt Hayley grab her by her leg and she looked down at her daughter. "He's gone," she said, then took a steadying breath. "And it's just you and me, kid."

E.J. WAS ON HIS WAY to his suite when Martin called on his cell phone. "Hey, Martin."

"I've been looking for you. I finally have some answers regarding that accident you asked me to look into."

He'd almost forgotten. "What did you come up with?"

"The man who hit Mrs. Flynn, Ken Row, seems to have quite a record of fender benders, and probably shouldn't be driving, but he's got money and he tends to get what he wants. His attorney takes care of his troubles, including this case."

"Who is the attorney?"

"Darrel Wise of Broad, Simpson and Wise. Wise is known to keep these things simple. No insurance, a settlement offer and a confidentiality statement."

"What are his plans for Mrs. Flynn?"

"Word is, Wise figures that since your friend doesn't have valid insurance, he's going to offer her a small settlement and count on the fact that she can't sue."

"How much?"

"Three thousand, injury and damage."

He grimaced. "So, he hits her, then pays

her off with peanuts because she can't fight him?"

"That's about it."

He had a memory of Sara's face when she realized that her car was probably totaled and felt a surge of emotion. And protectiveness. He'd told Mary that he wanted Sara to be safe. "Can he get away with it?"

"Sure. He's got all the leverage. It isn't as if he's dealing with someone like you."

E.J. exhaled, then knew what he had to do. "That's a good idea."

"What?"

"Let him deal with me," he said, and told Martin what he wanted him to do. Then he went to find Mrs. Stroud.

An hour later, E.J. walked back into the billiard room and found Sara sitting on the floor by her sleeping daughter. Sara looked up when he came in, and he was a bit relieved that she almost looked happy to see him. "I'm glad you're still here," he said, keeping his voice down.

She eased away from the child and stood as he came closer. "We straightened up.

She was so tired, I'm letting her take a nap before we go home," she said in a whisper.

"How about you?" he asked, taking in the faint shadows that smudged her eyes as she stood to face him, and that feeling of protectiveness he'd experienced an hour ago came back full force. "You look tired, too."

"I'm okay," she said, and he knew it was a lie. She brushed at her hair, tucking it behind her ears. "Did you need something?"

He wasn't going to think of what he really needed when he saw the way she touched her tongue to her full bottom lip. "Dinner," he said, and before she could refuse, he quickly said, "Here, now, just dinner. I asked the housekeeper to make up something simple, something for Hayley, and had her get a good bottle of wine." He kept talking quickly, afraid she'd shoot down the idea the minute he stopped. "Milk for Hayley. Chicken, salad, bread. Anything else you feel like. Or fast food, if you'd prefer. I can always send Andrew out for some burgers and shakes."

"I don't think a drive-through would be the thing to do in a limousine," she said.

He hoped he wasn't overplaying his hand. He reached in his pocket for his cell phone and said, "Then, in one minute, more or less, Mrs. Stroud is going to call and ask me where to serve dinner."

His phone rang right on cue but he didn't answer it. "What should I tell her?"

"Hayley's asleep."

"No problem." Then he flipped the phone open.

"Are you ready for dinner, sir?" Mrs. Stroud asked.

"Yes, we are. Serve it on the upper terrace, please. We'll be there in five minutes, and make up a place for a child to sleep on the floor. Blankets, pillows, whatever."

"Yes, sir," she said, and hung up.

"The upper terrace?" Sara asked.

"Yes. It's off my suite," he said.

He moved quickly, crouching by Hayley. "What's the best way to do this?" he asked.

Sara was beside him, brushing his shoulder with her thigh as she reached down and gently took a stuffed dog out of Sara's hand. "Get your hands under her and be careful," she whispered. "But do it quickly."

He managed to lift the little girl up and into his arms. She shifted for just a moment, then snuggled into his chest with complete trust. It unnerved him how tiny and trusting she was. He'd never carried a child before. He got to his feet carefully, then motioned for Sara to open the door.

They made their way through the house, neither of them talking until they'd reached the doors to his suite. He motioned to them. "In there."

She opened the doors and Mrs. Stroud came toward him.

Edward crossed to where blankets and pillows had been laid out on the floor just inside the doors. He eased Hayley down into the blankets and she instantly rolled onto her side, still asleep.

Once Sara had made sure her daughter was settled, he saw her smile.

"What's so amusing?" he asked, enjoying the way she looked when she seemed more relaxed.

"You."

"Me?"

"You, the man with no affinity for children, and you did that like an old pro."

"A first for me," he said, "believe it or not."

Sara looked at this man and knew she was actually looking forward to their meal. She looked around the luxurious room and then through the French doors to what must be the upper terrace.

"Is she okay there?" Edward asked, referring to Hayley.

"She…she's fine," she said.

"Dinner is ready, whenever you wish," Mrs. Stroud said in a low voice as she came back into the room. She was a pleasant-looking lady, in a loose-fitting dress on a slender frame, with short gray hair and deep brown eyes behind rimless glasses.

"Hungry?" Edward asked Sara.

Sara was hungry, very hungry. She couldn't remember whether or not she'd eaten today. "Yes, I am."

"Me, too," he murmured, and led the way out into the softness of the evening.

She followed him onto the terrace, a space decorated with wrought-iron furniture, gas lamps that cast the area in a gentle light and a hot tub that was covered with a safety top. It was wonderful, and in that moment she knew how easy it would be to just let herself slip into this fantasy. With Edward.

Then she looked at him, and knew she could do this. She could be with Edward. She could have dinner. They could talk. Then she would go back to her own world. Alone. With only this night to remember.

CHAPTER THIRTEEN

SARA SAT DOWN at the table and watched Edward pour white wine in her goblet. She felt a bit like Cinderella, as though she was being pampered.

They lifted their goblets and Sara sipped the cool, crisp wine, liking the way it made her feel. "I can't tell you how much the toys and games will mean to the kids on Saturday night," she murmured.

"Thank Mrs. Stroud," Edward said as he took another sip. "I wouldn't have known what to get."

"You were a kid once. Surely you haven't forgotten."

He looked down at the chicken breasts, salad, cold asparagus and French roll on his plate. "Well, it's been a while."

"You aren't exactly ancient," she said before tasting the wine again.

"Bordering on it."

"How old are you?" she asked, watching him over the rim of her glass.

"Thirty-nine. How about you?"

"Twenty-eight."

He lifted one eyebrow in her direction and slowly sipped his wine. Then he exhaled. "Let's see. When I was twenty-eight, I had maybe ten dollars in my pocket, a pickup truck that was on its last legs, and was looking for another job wildcatting in the oil fields."

She'd heard he was self-made, but she hadn't a clue that he'd ever been down and out. "You were broke?"

"Most of my life. My dad and I worked in the oil fields for as long as I can remember. When I was a kid I tagged along with him, and when I got old enough, I worked."

She motioned with her wineglass to the house. "Then how did this...how did you ever get this?"

"Luck, and timing," he said.

"Well, there's luck, then there's *luck,*" she said with a shake of her head. "But this is…extraordinary and hardly qualifies as luck."

"I stumbled onto something that could improve production and dependability in oil rigs. A little thing, but something no one else had thought of until then. It worked, and as they say, the rest is history."

"So, you built your company on it?"

"That and a few other things," he murmured.

She looked out at the pastures beyond the grounds of the house. "So you ended up living like a crown prince of some small country?"

"I told you, this was my accountant's idea."

"Oh, I forgot. A tax write-off. Some tax write-off," she murmured. "It's a perfect setting for the ball."

"I guess so," he said as he speared food with his fork.

"You're going to have a great time. You won't believe the program and the dinner and… You'll see, it'll be perfect, and you'll be right in the middle of it."

He shook his head. "No, I won't. I'll be there to lend my name, and that's all I'm doing."

She carefully speared pieces of asparagus with her fork and wondered why she'd forgotten how lovely sharing a meal could be. "That's not what I heard."

"What did you hear?"

"You're on the list for the auction," she said, then put a piece of asparagus in her mouth and reached for her roll.

"What list?"

She broke up her roll. "For the bachelor auction."

E.J. almost choked on his wine, coughed to clear his throat, then as he put his glass down, he asked, "What?"

"The bachelor auction. You know, where women bid on eligible men to spend the evening with them?" She sipped a bit of wine, then looked at him with mischief in her eyes. "You're on the block, Edward."

He sank back in his chair as he pressed the cloth napkin to his mouth. That wily old man! Ray had set him up. "So, I'm on the list, huh?"

"You sure are." She grinned at him. "Right at the top."

Ray was going to pay. "I'll take my name off of it," he muttered. The idea of being auctioned off made him sick.

"If you do, you'll be disappointing a lot of people. Your minimum bid is the highest on the list."

"My minimum bid? How much?" he asked.

"Two thousand dollars."

"Well, I'll give them twice that much not to do it," he said, his mind made up. Then he had a better idea. "Unless you'll bid?"

"Me?" That brought laughter this time. "I couldn't bid two dollars, let alone two thousand. Sorry," she said, and dug into her food. "You're on your own."

He watched her eat, enjoying the way the soft gas light caught at the highlights in her hair and thought the conversation about him being on the auction block was over. But he was wrong. "I wonder how much you'll go for at the auction?" she said.

"If I give you money, would you bid on me?" he asked.

"I won't be there. I'm watching the children. After they do a five-minute program at the beginning to thank the people for coming, they're being taken to the billiard room so the adults can have a party. Including the auction." She sipped the last of the wine and put the glass down. "This is really good wine. I don't drink very often, but even I know this is very nice."

He poured more for her. "Isn't there any way you can get out of working and be at the ball?"

"No, and besides, I wouldn't fit in," she said, and he watched the way her smile disappeared in the soft light.

"You'd fit just fine," he murmured, and knew that if he was going, he wanted her there. "We can work something out."

"No," she said quickly. "We can't work out anything. I'm there to handle the kids, and that's the way it should be." She pushed her plate back slightly. "And you'll be auctioned off to the highest bidder." She grinned at him. "I do hope someone takes pictures of that."

A low crying sound came from the

house and Sara was on her feet immediately. She hurried inside, and when he got there, she was crouched over Hayley, brushing at her fair hair, talking to her softly. Then the child turned over, curled into a small ball and sighed deeply. E.J. just watched. The tenderness in her dealings with her daughter touched him. He liked the way she hummed softly, then lowered her hand to rub light circles over her daughter's back. In a matter of moments, Hayley was asleep again, and Sara bent to kiss her.

She stood and moved toward him. "I think it's time for us to get going," she said, but at the same time, took a step closer.

E.J. couldn't help himself. He leaned down and tasted her, savoring the sweetness of her parted lips. He wrapped his arms around her and pulled her close. He skimmed her cheek with his fingertips, then ran his hand through her silky hair.

Just when he was losing himself in the moment, there was a sound. He looked down and found himself staring right into the sleepy face of Hayley. She wasn't screaming or crying. She simply reached out and pushed his leg. "Mommy?" she said.

Sara bent down and reached for Hayley. E.J. left Sara with her daughter while he went outside and out of sight. He stood there for a long time, waiting for his heart-rate to settle, and tried to figure out how he could have let himself get so swept up with Sara when her daughter was asleep in the same room.

He could hear Sara talking in a low voice to her daughter, then she was behind him. "I think I need to leave, but... could I call a cab or something? I know I haven't had much to drink, but I'd rather be on the safe side." He turned and she was a few feet from him with Hayley on her hip. He thought her lips looked a bit swollen from the kisses, but he could have been imagining it.

"I'll call Andrew, and he can take you home."

She didn't argue. "Thanks."

Hayley twisted in Sara's arm, looked at E.J. and suddenly held out her arms for him to take her. "You're going home," he said, but that didn't stop her from throwing herself toward him and almost out of her mother's arms. He caught her, and as soon as he had a hold on her, she put a tiny arm around his neck.

What was it with these females that they brought out the craziest responses in him? He actually liked the tiny arm going around his neck, and those blue eyes staring into his. "Get toys?" she asked.

"Toys? Sure, why not?" he said, and crossed to the house phone and told Andrew to bring the car around to the front entrance.

"I need her car seat," Sara said.

"Could you please get the car seat out of the car parked at the service entrance and put it in the limo," he told Andrew, then hung up and looked at Sara. "Let's get her some toys from downstairs to take with her," he said, and headed out of the room.

They made their way to the billiard room and he set Hayley on the ground. "Get a toy to take with you."

As soon as she'd reached the toys, E.J.

turned to look at Sara. She was staring at the floor. "Sara? I'm sorry."

She looked at him then, but her eyes were shadowed and unreadable. "I wanted to kiss you," she murmured.

"No, I'm sorry for getting so caught up with Hayley in the room. I totally forgot she was there."

"I did, too." She grimaced. Hayley was back with a stuffed animal in each hand. "Just one," Sara said.

"Let her take them both," E.J. said.

Sara hesitated, then said, "Okay, this once." Hayley grinned at her mother, and E.J. noticed the way the child's eyes crinkled up like her mother's. "Now we have to get home."

Sara picked up Hayley and the three of them walked to the front door. The car was waiting. "Andrew's here," he said. He wanted to say he'd ride with them, but he knew that wasn't a good idea. "You can get Mary's car later?"

"Sure," Sara said, going ahead of him down the stairs.

She opened the back door to the limo

and ducked in to put Hayley in the car seat. Then she turned to him. "Thanks" was all she said, then got inside. The door closed and Andrew drove off with Sara and Hayley.

He felt oddly isolated once the two of them had left, and that feeling shook him a bit. He'd never really regretted any woman leaving before, but that was exactly how he felt at that moment. This situation was a lot more complicated than he'd ever thought it could be, and for the first time he realized just how entangled a man could get with a woman.

He started back inside when his cell phone rang. "Hello?"

"Hey, Sonny, it's me," Ray said with irritating cheerfulness.

"Just the man I wanted to talk to," he said as he sank down on the top step by the open door.

"Is that good or bad?" Ray asked, a bit hesitantly.

He debated how to express his anger, then figured out exactly how to get even with the old man. "I was thinking about the ball, and I decided that you should come. You'd have a great time, and I know how you love to dance."

"Why did you change your mind?" Ray asked, a touch of suspicion in his voice.

"I'm not going to get dressed up in a monkey suit by myself. You owe it to me to be there and be in a tux."

Ray laughed. "Now, that sounds like fun. Lots of good food, and pretty ladies. Maybe you'll get lucky."

"Maybe you will," he said.

Ray laughed again. "Let's concentrate on you, Sonny."

"Don't call me Sonny," he muttered out of habit, although he was actually smiling at the idea of Ray in a tux at the ball, not knowing what was about to hit him.

"Sure thing, Sonny. I'll be down there tomorrow."

"Great. Now, what did you need?"

"Nothing. I just wanted to see how you were doing. I wasn't expecting you to go back to Houston until the ball."

"Me neither," E.J. said, and hung up.

E.J. stood, then went back into the house, smiling.

THE STRAINS OF THE STRING quartet drifted out of the open French doors along the side of the ballroom, filtering into the soft summer night. Sara heard the music and was drawn to it. She went out the side door of the billiard room where the kids were having the time of their lives. The volunteers had things under control, and Sara couldn't resist a peek at the festivities.

When she'd gone into the ballroom two hours earlier with the children to do their program, she'd felt as if she'd stepped into a fantasy land of sparkling crystal, jewels and furs, of women in long gowns, men in tuxes and the sound of laughter everywhere. Lindsey and Zane Holden led the festivities, Lindsey in a simple white gown that showed her pregnancy and complimented her glow. Amy Gallagher, the director of the center, was there with her husband, Quint, carrying their infant and proudly watching Taylor, their daughter, sing a nursery rhyme. Anthony, Matt and Brittany's boy, showed off the painting the kids had done.

Five minutes, not much more, then the children's part was over, and they were taken to the billiard room and into their fantasy land, leaving the adults to their enchanted evening. Mary was thrilled. The guests were generous and the evening was running smoothly. Sara loved to watch the kids having fun, and she was happy that the money raised would exceed expectations. But part of her felt oddly left out.

A stupid reaction, but one that began the moment she'd spotted Edward coming into the ballroom. She'd seen him at the center since the evening of their dinner and he'd backed off. He'd been funny and joking—he'd actually played with Hayley, tossing stuffed toys with her—and when she'd look up, he'd be watching her. But they hadn't had any more time alone. She didn't know if she was relieved or disappointed. But seeing him come into the ballroom made her heart beat faster.

People flocked around him and the older man he was with. The man was more compact than Edward, with short gray hair, but the same smile and gait. He had to be Ray, his father, whom Edward had told her was coming. They both were laughing, nodding, shaking hands, and they fit in completely, despite Edward's hesitation at appearing at the event. Camera people were everywhere, snapping shots of the guests, surrounding Edward, taking more pictures than were necessary.

Then Edward had spotted her. But all he'd done was smile, and then he disappeared. Once she'd made sure the children were settled, she'd stepped outside onto the terrace. She quietly approached the ballroom from the open doors and peeked inside.

Couples twirled around the dance floor, then the music stopped and she heard Lindsey's voice come over the speakers. "Now for the last bachelor in the auction this evening. The main event."

There was applause and laughter, and she leaned forward a bit to watch. "We saved the best for last, a true bachelor, handsome, bright, and he looks like a dream in a tux." More laughter and enthusiastic applause, and Lindsey motioned to the crowd. "Come on. You can't back down now." The applause grew, and Lindsey said, "Ladies, Mr. Sommers!"

The guests were blocking her view, and all Sara could see was Lindsey with the microphone in her hand, laughing. "Don't be shy," she said. Edward said something that she couldn't make out, then Lindsey laughed and said, "Of course. Come on up here. Your starting bid is the highest of the night."

People applauded in encouragement, and she wondered if Edward was running in the opposite direction. Then she watched as Edward made his way through the glittering crowd, and Lindsey held out her hand.

"Sara?"

She spun around at the sound of Edward's voice. Edward? She turned back to the barroom and saw his Dad stepping up onto the stage with Lindsey. He was smiling, but it was tight and she could tell he wasn't happy. Then she turned back to Edward. "What are you doing out here? I thought you were—"

"Ray's taking my place, and he deserves it." He was smiling a bit smugly. "I thought this was a good payback for him offering me up like that."

She could barely take it in, him in the tux, standing not more than two feet from her. "But it's you, you're supposed to be up there."

"That's what Ray was hoping for, but I figured as long as they had a Sommers, they wouldn't mind." His smile grew. "He's a bachelor, and quite a catch." He looked past her. "They're bidding," he said, coming closer as she turned around to look into the room. He rested his hands on her shoulders. "Who's bidding?" he asked near her ear.

"I don't know," she whispered, closing her eyes tightly to fight her reaction to his closeness.

"Wow," he whispered by her ear. "Who would have thought it?"

She opened her eyes, heard cheering and applause, then she saw Mary step up onto the stage. Mary? And Lindsey was saying, "Five thousand dollars! What a wonderful contribution!"

"Mary bid on your dad?" she said.

"Looks that way," he murmured. "I wonder where Robert is?"

As Mary and Ray stepped off the stage together, the music started again and Sara turned. "Your poor dad." He was inches from her.

"He came out of that smelling like a rose," he said. "I was hoping for someone who would…" He shrugged. "Mary's too good for him." His hazel eyes flicked over Sara's plain black dress, with its off-the-shoulder neckline and the skirt down to her knees. A very plain dress, but he smiled at her. "Dance with me?"

"Oh, no, I'm not…"

"Not in there," he said. "I don't want to go into that crowd again. Come on," he said.

She didn't move. "Where?"

He reached out to take her hand. His

fingers curled around hers, and he smiled. She couldn't resist and found herself moving silently around the back of the house and upstairs to the upper terrace. He pulled her into his arms and began to move slowly to the music.

At first she couldn't move, the feeling of being in his arms all but riveted her to the spot. Then he leaned down, brushing her ear with his lips. "Please?" he whispered, and she leaned into him, giving up her resistance.

They moved together, swaying to the soft strains of an old tune that she barely remembered. A slow, sensuous tune. Sara closed her eyes and moved with Edward, and she felt just like Cinderella must have at the ball. Glitter and riches, Prince Charming. She felt him kiss her loose hair, then his hand slipped to the small of her back and drew her closer. "Great music," he whispered.

"Hmm." She sighed, and found herself wishing that this night could go on forever. To not have to think, to not have to worry about the future. Just focus on the here and now, on the two of them.

But the music didn't go on forever. It ended softly, then there was a burst of distant applause, people talking, laughing, and more music, a faster song. But it was as if nothing had changed. Edward held her to him and kept moving, humming softly near her ear. His hand moved slowly on her back, brushing her skin with heat, lingering at her waist.

"I should be helping with the children and you should be in there," she whispered, but didn't let go or stop.

"I'm where I want to be." It was he who stopped then. He cupped her chin, bringing her face up to meet his gaze. His eyes were shadowed by the night and the gas lamps, but she felt the intensity there, an intensity that echoed in her. She trembled slightly, and when Edward ducked his head, she met him. Their lips touching, almost tentatively, maybe even uncertainly, and then she went to him.

There was an ache deep inside Sara and the only way to ease it was by being close to Edward. She knew that in her soul, and she didn't hesitate. Once, just once, she'd drop her guard with him. And no one would get hurt. She would simply walk away when he said it was time. It was okay, she told herself. It was okay. It didn't have to be forever.

CHAPTER FOURTEEN

THE MAGIC OF the night was all around as Sara clung to Edward, wrapped in his arms. She heard the distant music, the sounds of the party, but her world shrank to this man, this moment. She was exquisitely aware of everything about him, the hollow at his throat, the line of his jaw. His kisses warmed her skin, trailing from her lips to her throat, then settling at the sensitive hollow by her ear.

He pulled back slightly and she looked up at him, reached out to touch her fingers to his chin, and she trembled. "Please," she whispered, and circled his neck with her arms. "Please kiss me again."

He didn't hesitate. He lowered his head and kissed her long and deep. She had never experienced anything like this before. It was beyond anything she could have imagined, that sense of belonging right here, in this man's arms. She was home, finally, she was home. In that moment, she knew that she loved him. Never had she loved like this. Holding on tight, afraid to break the contact, she hoped this feeling of complete happiness never ended.

E.J. SAT ON ONE of the terrace chairs, holding Sara in her lap, listening to the music in the distance. Her cheek was pressing against his chest, his arm around her waist. He could feel the warmth of her through his shirt, and inhaled her delicious scent. A scent that was hers alone. Sweet and gentle. He stared into the shadows of the terrace with the knowledge of where this relationship was headed.

Ray had been right. When you found that one person, you knew it. It had just taken him longer than most to figure things out. He pressed a kiss to her forehead and felt her stir against him. Being with her felt so right. It was so simple, yet so monumental. He loved her.

She shifted, looking up at him.

He met her eyes. "Dance?" he asked as the music drifted out to them.

She laughed softly, snuggling closer to him. "No, I don't think so," she murmured.

"Good," he said, and leaned down, kissing her quickly and fiercely before pulling back.

"We should get back," she said, her hand on his chest, resting over his heart.

"No, we shouldn't, not just yet. I want to…" He kissed her again, gathering the courage to say to this woman what he never had in his entire life. "We need to talk," he finally said.

She touched his lips with her finger, hushing him, before she said, "Not now, not now," and she wrapped her arms around his neck, pulling him down for a kiss.

He didn't fight it, both of them reaching out to the other and experiencing emotions Edward had never thought possible.

But with Sara, those feelings were there instantly. One touch, the feel of her in his arms, and they were there. He'd joked about Ray's idea of love, but in that moment, he knew that Ray had been dead on. He felt Sara, deep in his soul.

When their kiss ended, E.J. sank back into the chair, holding her close, feeling her heart beating in unison with his. "I was thinking..." he started, but stopped when his security beeper went off.

He looked at it, and saw 911 displayed. A security breach. He looked down at Sara, not letting her go. "I need to see to this. There might be a problem."

"Oh, sure," she murmured, and he reached for his cell phone to call security. "You've been looking for me?" he asked.

"Sir, there's a man on the grounds, and he hasn't been cleared. He claims to know someone at the ball and has to see her."

"Who is he looking for?" E.J. asked, rubbing his hand slowly up and down Sara's arm.

"Mrs. Flynn. Someone said that they saw her with you."

"Who is it?"

"He says he's her husband, Paul Flynn."

E.J. glanced at Sara, at the way her cheeks were flushed and her lips swollen from his kisses. Then he met her gaze. "Where are you?" he asked the security man.

"Outside the main kitchen, by the caterer's truck."

"I'll be there in five minutes. Keep things quiet, okay?"

"Yes, sir."

E.J. put the phone down, then set Sara on her feet and got up. There was no way he could tell her that Paul was here, not until he knew what was going on. "Sorry, there's a problem I need to see to."

"What kind of problem? It's not with the ball, is it?"

"No, it's probably nothing, but they want me to be sure."

"A party crasher?"

"Could be," he murmured. Sara touched his arm.

"Should I wait, or—"

He reached out and caressed her cheek. "Wait. Okay?"

"Okay," she echoed, and he bent to kiss her quickly before pulling back. "Five minutes," he said, and left.

Sara sat back down, feeling as though, for once in her life, she was where she should be. She could trust herself. Edward was Edward. He wasn't Paul. He never could be. She'd take things slowly, but knew her life had changed forever.

Edward's cell phone rang, startling her. He'd set it on the table and walked off without it. It kept ringing, so she finally answered. "Yes?"

"Mr. Sommers, please?"

"He's not here right now."

"Oh, this is Security. He just called."

"Oh, yes, he's on his way."

"Good, we weren't sure if we should call the police or not. This guy's getting a bit weird. He keeps saying that he's going to find his wife."

"His wife?"

"Mrs. Flynn. That's all he'll say."

She went cold. "What's his name?"

"Paul Flynn."

If she hadn't been sitting down, she would have fallen over. Paul? Sickness rose in her throat. "Where is he?"

"Outside the service entrance."

She hung up, her hands shaking, and something hit her with a sickening thud. Edward knew. He'd known when he'd left, and he'd lied to her. She hurried across the terrace to doors leading back inside. Things never changed. Never.

As she raced past the ballroom, she heard someone call her name.

She turned and saw Mr. Row, the man who had hit her car, standing there with a stranger. "I thought it was you," the elderly man said. "What a coincidence, but then, I guess I shouldn't be surprised."

Well, she was certainly surprised to see him. Then she looked at the man to his right—and felt as if she was having a full-blown nightmare. The man from the restaurant, the man she'd dumped food on, was not only standing by Mr. Row in a tuxedo, but he was smiling at her. "This is Mr. Wise, my attorney," the elderly man said. "We're here for the ball."

"Oh, yes," she breathed. "Your attorney."

The blond man nodded, obviously having no idea who she was. "I was going to call and make an appointment for the discussions on the settlement."

She couldn't even think about that. "Okay, sure," she said, ready to bolt. But Mr. Row stopped her by placing a hand on her shoulder. "Mrs. Flynn, I have to say that the settlement would have been a good one, even if Mr. Sommers's attorney hadn't stepped in."

She knew her mouth dropped. "What?"

"Mr. Griggs, his attorney. Mr. Wise would have made you a handsome settlement without the interference."

Edward had forced the man to make a good settlement? The sick feeling worsened. Manipulating and lying. She felt as if her world was exploding around her. "I need to go," she said in a rush, and turned to hurry away from the two men.

She'd thought she loved Edward. No, she did love him, she admitted as she hurried around the side of the house. That was her problem. Another mistake, but this mistake was worse. Then she saw the service entrance, lights on, trucks, Mary's car, and men standing near the house.

She heard the men talking, not loudly, but she could tell it wasn't a cordial conversation. Then she saw Edward. Standing beside him was Paul, being restrained by a security guard. Paul, with his long dark hair pulled back in a ponytail, several days' worth of beard, jeans and a numbingly psychedelic shirt. Her heart sank.

"What's going on here?" she asked.

They turned at the sound of her voice, the guards, then Edward, and then Paul.

Paul looked surprised, then smiled at her. "Hi, babe," he drawled. "I finally found you. Now, tell these cretins to get their hands off me."

She couldn't move. She just stood there, staring at him. "What are you doing here?"

"Looking for you," he said, coming over to her as Security released him. His smile gave her the chills. "I found out you were staying in Houston. The guy at the restaurant where you work said you were at some fancy ball out here. So, I came running. I wasn't going to wait on your stoop all night."

She was aware of Edward standing behind Paul, but she couldn't look at him. "What did he do?" she asked in a tight voice.

A guard stepped forward and said, "Ma'am, he is on the property illegally. He said he's your husband."

"My ex-husband," she murmured, never taking her eyes off Paul.

"Did you ask him here?" the guard asked.

"No, I didn't."

She saw Paul's expression tighten a bit. "Now, love, you know that you want me here. We haven't seen each other for—"

"Three months and six days," she said numbly.

"You're keeping track," he said. He came toward her and made to touch her.

"Don't touch me," she ground out.

He did as she asked. "We've had some disagreements," Paul was saying, obviously explaining himself to the others. "But I'm here to visit my little girl. I can't tell you how upset I was when I found out that she'd taken my daughter out of state without my permission. All the way from Illinois."

"You weren't around," she said. "I couldn't find you anywhere."

He turned to her. "All you had to do was call me," he said. "You violated our custody agreement."

"No," she said, the horror growing. She watched as Edward moved closer to her and Paul. It made Sara sick to think she'd ever believed anything Paul said, anything either of them said.

"Sara," Edward said, coming over to her, taking her hand in his, but she jerked back.

"You knew he was here, and you lied to me. And you lied about the car and the settlement you seemed to have arranged for my accident!"

He stared at her as if she'd dealt him a blow to the middle. "I can explain."

She clasped her hands tightly together, trying to ignore the pain she felt in her heart. "Stand in line behind Paul. He can explain, too."

Paul was watching them carefully. "Hey,

you two know each other? I thought you were just working here," he said to Sara.

Edward glared at him, and Sara shot him a withering look. "I'm working here, Paul," she muttered.

Then Edward spoke. "What do you want, Sara?"

"I want you all gone," she breathed with aching truth. "And I want to leave."

"Well, I'd love to go," Paul said. "But I'm broke, and I haven't seen my little girl yet."

Her hands were almost numb from clenching them so hard. "I don't have any money, Paul, none. And you can't just pop into Hayley's life when you need something."

He shrugged and gave her a slimy-looking smile. "I told you, I can't leave, so that means that I'll be sticking around for a while, and that means that I'll get to know my little Hayley."

Sickness rose in her throat. "Paul, please…"

The security guard spoke to Edward. "Sir, what are we going to do?"

"It's up to Mrs. Flynn," he said.

"Ma'am, we can arrest him for trespassing, we can escort him off the property, he can stay with you, or you can both leave."

Edward could feel the foundations of the world he'd just started to build shaking ominously. Sara had her eyes closed tightly, and she was deathly white. Paul just looked smug. If he was alone with the man, he'd have a lot more to say.

She opened her eyes and looked at him. It was then he knew that he'd do whatever it took to make her happy. Anything. He looked at the security men. "Keep him here for a minute," he said, then looked at Sara. "Come with me."

She drew back. "I'm leaving."

He wasn't going to play it safe anymore. "You can do whatever you want, but I really need you to come with me for a minute."

She hesitated, literally swaying from side to side, then she exhaled. "Okay."

They went around the side of the house and Paul called after her, "Hey, don't leave me here with these goons!"

Once they were out of sight of the others, E.J. stopped and turned to Sara. "What can I say? I was trying to help? I didn't want him hurting you anymore. I thought I could…" He shrugged. "I thought I could protect you. I'm sorry. I was wrong."

She stared at the ground and he could barely see her breathing. "You were wrong," she whispered.

"I was. I know it. And arranging a settlement, that was gut instinct. I knew you were broke and needed a car. That protection thing again. This is all new to me."

She looked at him then. "What is?"

He hesitated, then put his life on the line. "Loving you."

She stared at him, unblinking, then he saw her start to shake. "No."

"Oh, yes, love, yes." He touched her then, brushing at her cheek, so soft and silky. "I love you. Go figure. I never believed in it until now."

She still didn't move. He didn't know what to say or do, but he felt as if everything he was or would be was hanging in the balance. "Did you hear me?" he asked.

She nodded, then her hand reached out and touched his chest. She pressed her hand palm down above his heart. "I hear you."

There was a blood-curdling scream, and Sara jerked toward the sound. She took off, and he went after her, around the house and back to the group. But now Paul was in an armlock and the security guard was telling him to shut up. "What's going on?" E.J. asked as he caught up to Sara.

"These idiots are gearing you up for a huge lawsuit, man," Paul muttered.

Edward nodded to Security. "Let him go."

They released him, and Paul brushed off his clothes with great show, then looked at E.J. "Can the three of us talk without your goons around?"

He looked at Sara, then at the security men. "Go ahead. It's okay."

"What do you want—" the main man started, but Edward cut him off.

"No, just leave us. We'll work this out."

The two men nodded and left. Now it was just the three of them. E.J. turned to

Sara and said, "Listen to me and understand what I'm saying, and above all, believe me."

She looked so tiny and fragile now. Her skin was pale and her eyes overly bright and he had no idea what she was thinking. But when he reached for her hand this time, she let him take it. She didn't hold on to him, but she didn't pull back, and it made his heart ache. Then he looked at Paul. "You listen to me. Sara isn't alone now. I will back her on anything she wants, from throwing you out of here feetfirst, locking you up or just letting you go. But get one thing straight. You're dealing with me if you do anything to hurt her, or to hurt Hayley."

Paul took a step toward him, the smile gone now and a cutting look in his eyes. "Big man, huh? You got money, so you think you rule the world. That kid is mine. And I'll do whatever I want, any time I want to do it, with Hayley..." He looked at Sara. "And with her. Unless she's married to you..." He flicked his eyes down to

Sara's hands. "And it doesn't look that way. Therefore, you don't have a say in this."

E.J. felt Sara try to pull free of his hand, but he didn't let her. He looked Paul in the eyes and spoke honestly, and from the heart. "I'm in this because I love Sara." He felt Sara grow completely still, and he didn't look at her. He was watching Paul, who went from belligerent to assessing in one fell swoop. "You're up against the two of us."

"Well, big man, since you have all the money and this is your place, you can kick me out, but if you do, I won't go alone. I'm taking the kid with me."

E.J. heard Sara gasp, and he moved, switching from holding her hand to putting his arm around her shoulders to pull her against him. She was shaking and it tore at him. "No, you're not," she gasped. "You can't, Paul."

He eyed her narrowly. "Are you going to make it worth my while to walk out?"

E.J. understood completely. "You'd sell your child, just like that?"

Paul had the decency to look a bit

abashed, but it didn't last for long. "She'd be better off without me around."

"That's the first thing you've said that's actually true," E.J. said.

"Sonny, what in the heck's going on out here?"

Ray approached E.J., and he wasn't alone. Martin was with him, after probably being alerted by Security, and Mary was there carrying Hayley. The child looked up, saw Sara and smiled, then she looked over at Paul and the smile died. She stared at him, then said in a tiny voice. "Daddy?"

"Yeah, sunshine, it's me," Paul said with a grin, and came toward Mary, putting his hands out to take Hayley. But the child held on to Mary, not letting go. "Come on, sunshine, come to Daddy."

Hayley shook her head. "No," she said, and looked at Sara, then lurched toward her mother. "Mommy!"

Sara moved quickly, scooping up her daughter, and held her tightly against her chest, as if she could shield her from Paul. But he was persistent. "Hey, it's me. Daddy. Come on. We'll have some fun."

The little girl lifted her face from her mother's neck, looked at Paul, and that was when E.J. realized that she had a small wooden block in her hand. Before anyone could react she threw it hard at Paul, catching him on the bridge of the nose and making him yelp with pain. He grabbed his face, and E.J. saw blood seeping out between his fingers.

He would have given the kid a medal if it all wasn't so pitiful. Then Paul became enraged. "You little brat, look what you did!"

Hayley's bottom lip trembled, then she let out a scream to rival all screams right before she buried her face in Sara's neck.

That was it. E.J. could no longer stand around and watch. He made his move, grabbing Paul by the arm before he knew what was happening. "Ray, help me get him some medical aid," he said to his dad.

"Sure thing, Sonny, bring him on over to the porch and I'll find something to fix him good."

Mary moved toward Sara and the crying child, and let Ray and E.J. all but drag the man over to the porch. E.J. pushed him down on the step, sent Ray in to get a cloth, and he hunkered down in front of the other man. He kept his voice low. "Look at me," he ground out.

E.J. was ready to make a deal with Paul, to permanently get him out of Sara and Hayley's life, and start his own future with both mother and daughter.

CHAPTER FIFTEEN

PAUL SLOWLY RAISED his head. A cut slashed across the bridge of his nose, bleeding profusely and dripping down onto the ground and his jeans. "I'm suing," he muttered.

"Who, your own child?"

"Oh, for the—"

"Listen to me, you scum. You're going to leave, and you're going to walk out of Sara's and Hayley's lives, and unless you get a whole personality transplant that includes a chip for being a decent human being and caring father, you aren't coming back."

"Says who?"

"Says me. And my money. And my power." For the first time he could remember, he relished his position. "And my staff of attorneys, who, if I ask them to, will look at your life under a microscope, and every dirty little secret that you think you've hidden will become national news."

That piqued Paul's interest. E.J. could see it in his eyes, along with fear. "So let's make a deal," he muttered.

E.J. glanced to his left where Martin stood, silently watching. Then Ray came out the door carrying a white towel and a single Band-aid. "This was all I could find, Sonny."

"Good enough," he said.

"So, what do I do now? I have no money," Paul said, his voice muffled by the terry cloth.

E.J. looked up at Martin and asked, "How much do you have in your wallet?"

Martin shook his head. "This is extortion at best and blackmail at worst."

"How much?"

"Six, seven hundred."

He looked at his father. "How much do you have, Dad?"

"A couple of hundred."

E.J. held out his hand. "Give it to me," he said.

Martin gave him some bills, then Ray, and E.J. held them in his hand as he looked at Paul. "Take this and get out of here. Understood?"

Paul looked at the money, then grabbed it. E.J. stood and looked around. He saw the security man hanging back, not intruding until he motioned to him. "He's ready to leave. Get him in your car, then take him to the bus, or the plane or the train station and buy him a one-way ticket anywhere he wants to go. Understand?"

"Yes, sir," the man said.

Paul glared at E.J., but didn't fight it any longer. He left with Security, obviously giving no thought to what he'd just walked away from.

E.J. crossed back to Sara. "He's gone."

Sara felt as if she were standing in a void, in a place where she didn't feel or sense anything. She knew she had Hayley in her arms, and when Mary offered to take her, she let her go. Then she stood there, without a clue what to do now. Ray and Mary went inside with Hayley, and Martin said something in a low voice to E.J. before he nodded and left. Then it was just she and E.J.

She looked at him, wondering how everything could have gone so wrong. "I'm sorry," she managed to say. "I'm so sorry, and I'll pay you back."

He was right in front of her. "Come with me," he said, and took her arm, leading her to his suite. Then he turned to her, cupping her chin in his hand. "Did you hear what I said to you before?"

She'd heard so much, but she didn't believe any of it. "Sure," she whispered. "He's gone. You paid him."

"Sara, I love you, and I love Hayley, and if you'll have me, I want to marry you."

She heard the words, but they didn't sink in. She bit her lip, hating the burn of tears behind her eyes. "Don't do this," she begged.

He drew her to him, and she clung to him one last time. "Sara, love, I mean it. I didn't have a clue what I wanted in my life until I saw you. And believe it or not, Hayley, too. I never met anyone who lit up my life, who changed my world just by being there. I never thought that a child would work her way into my heart." His hold on her was a bit unsteady as he whispered, "I love you, Sara Flynn. I want you…and Hayley, to marry me."

The words were starting to hit her, to filter through her being, and she was terrified to believe them. "But we can't…"

"If you can't trust me, if there isn't something in you that knows that this is real, we're lost…both of us." She thought she saw fear in his eyes, a fear that echoed in her when she thought about losing him and everything he'd brought into her life. Maybe for once this was something that could last.

"Do you think it could really happen?" she asked.

"Yes, I do," he said. "We'll play it by ear and work out everything as we go along." He hesitated, then drew back, his fingertip lifting her face up to his. "But it all depends on you, if you love me enough to trust me and let me be there for you. And for Hayley."

"What about Paul?" She shuddered. "He'll be back. He...he never leaves forever."

"Then we'll take care of him...together, and I promise you, he won't hurt you or Hayley ever again. Trust me."

Finally, for the first time in her life, she'd done something very right. She'd met Edward, and in that moment, she knew that she trusted him with her life and with Hayley's. "Oh, Edward," she breathed. "I love you. Yes, I love you."

"And do you trust me enough to marry me?"

She looked into his eyes and said, "Oh, yes, I do. I most certainly do."

He kissed her quickly, joyously, then drew back. "Is Hayley okay with Mary?"

"Just fine."

The music in the distance drifted into

the room, and Edward whispered, "Then can I have this dance?"

She smiled up at him a bit unsteadily. "I don't want to dance now. But maybe later," she said.

"Much later," Edward breathed as he wrapped his arms around her and pulled her into a kiss full of promise and love.

* * * * *

REQUEST YOUR FREE BOOKS!
2 FREE WHOLESOME ROMANCE NOVELS
IN LARGER PRINT
PLUS 2
FREE
MYSTERY GIFTS

✼✼✼✼✼✼✼✼✼✼✼✼✼✼✼✼✼✼✼✼✼✼✼

HEARTWARMING™

❋❋❋❋❋❋❋❋❋❋❋❋❋❋❋❋❋❋❋❋❋❋❋

Wholesome, tender romances

HWDIR13

LARGER-PRINT BOOKS!

GET 2 FREE LARGER-PRINT NOVELS PLUS 2 FREE MYSTERY GIFTS

Love Inspired

Larger-print novels are now available...

YES! Please send me the *Cowboy at Heart* collection in Larger Print. This collection begins with 3 FREE books and 2 FREE gifts in the first shipment, and more free gifts will follow! My books will arrive in 8 monthly shipments until I have the entire 51-book *Cowboy at Heart* collection. I will receive 2 or 3 FREE books in each shipment and I will pay just $4.99 U.S./ $5.89 CDN. for each of the other four books in each shipment, plus $2.99 for shipping and handling.* If I decide to keep the entire collection, I'll have paid for only 32 books because 19 books are FREE! I understand that by accepting the 3 free books and gifts places me under no obligation to buy anything. I can always return a shipment and cancel at any time. My free books and gifts are mine to keep no matter what I decide.

256 HCN 0779   456 HCN 0779

Name _____ (PLEASE PRINT) _____

Address _____ Apt. # _____

City _____ State/Prov. _____ Zip/Postal Code _____

Signature (if under 18, a parent or guardian must sign)

Mail to the **Harlequin® Reader Service:**
IN U.S.A.: P.O. Box 1867, Buffalo, NY 14240-1867
IN CANADA: P.O. Box 609, Fort Erie, Ontario L2A 5X3

ReaderService.com

Manage your account online!
- Review your order history
- Manage your payments
- Update your address

---

*We've designed
the Harlequin® Reader Service
website just for you.*

Enjoy all the features!
- Reader excerpts from any series
- Respond to mailings and special monthly offers
- Discover new series available to you
- Browse the Bonus Bucks catalog
- Share your feedback

Visit us at:

ReaderService.com